To Lucy!

Hope you enjoy
the book.

God bless,

Jue

FINDING AMELIA

Jane Amelia Smith

WESTBOW
PRESS
A DIVISION OF THOMAS NELSON

Finding Amelia

WestBow Press books may be ordered through booksellers or by contacting:

WestBow Press
A Division of Thomas Nelson
1663 Liberty Drive
Bloomington, IN 47403
www.westbowpress.com
1-(866) 928-1240

ISBN: 978-1-4497-3594-4 (sc)

Library of Congress Control Number: 2011963338

Printed in the United States of America

WestBow Press rev. date: 04/26/2012

You touched my soul, thank you!

Fred Budenbender – August 18, 2005

Connie Orcutt Block – January 16, 2007

Richard W. Smith – April 4, 2007

"Well done, good and faithful servant."
Matthew 25:23

Contents

Chapter 1

An Imperfect World

With passion bordering on ferocity, Amelia's fingers flew across the keys of the family's Steinway piano. Upon completion of *Mozart's piano concerto No. 15,* her shoulders slumped in frustration and her long dark locks cascaded onto the keys. To her amazement the instrument of her joy had somehow become nothing more than a relentless taskmaster.

The girl regained her composure at the sound of her father's soothing voice echoing from the doorway of the music room. "Amelia, always at it! I heard you playing and I thought maybe we could play a little ragtime before I leave to catch my train? Why are you still in your pajamas?"

"Oh Dad, I am not feeling myself today. I think I may have picked up this bug that is going around in school. I thought that I might just chill out for the rest of the day. I just wanted to get my early morning practice out of the way; I can't seem to get the last few notes right!"

"Well, maybe you are trying too hard. Let's get a little low brow and practice our ragtime, shall we?"

"Dad, I really don't feel much like playing the piano any longer. Maybe we could play together tomorrow." Amelia grimaced, sensing her dad's disappointment.

"Well, okay. We will have all the time in the world to exercise that old piano when you are feeling better. As we speak, Mom is in the kitchen making us some breakfast; I will let her know that you need some doctoring." Ken Morelli gently kissed his daughter on the top of her head.

"Oh Dad, will you be home early tonight for dinner?"

"Well, that is the plan; am I forgetting about something?"

Amelia hesitated. "Oh, no, I just wanted to run a few things by both you and Mom; nothing earth shattering. At least I hope not."

"Honey, are you sure that you are alright, other than the bug that has gotten you down?"

"I'll be fine, Dad; see you tonight." As her father walked from the room, Amelia blew him a kiss.

"Thanks honey. Okay, I better get breakfast or I'll miss my train. Love you!"

"Me too. Bye Dad."

In anticipation, Amelia waited for the sound of her mother's voice. During her fourteen years of life with two adoring parents, she had come to realize both the benefits as well as the demands placed upon the proverbial "perfect" only child.

"Amelia baby, Dad tells me you are under the weather."

Before Amelia could respond, Karen Morelli scooted beside her daughter on the oversized piano bench. "Let me look at you!"

"Oh Mom, don't start fussing over me; I just have a little bug."

"Well, all bugs are little; you just have to take them to task before they become big." Karen's hand automatically found its way to Amelia's forehead. "You don't feel like you have a fever, why don't you try to eat something with us."

"I will eat later, Mom; I just don't feel like it right now. You and Dad go to work. I will relax and be just fine. Oh, Dad said he would be home for dinner tonight, I hope we will be eating at home."

"Yes dear, in fact I was going to cook up one of Dad's favorites, Chicken Marsala. Maybe I should make you something lighter?"

Amelia rolled her eyes. "Really, Mom, you don't have to do that, I should be fine by this evening."

"Well, okay, call me at the library if you need anything. Maybe call your Granny Lou, she always cheers you up. I'm sure she would be willing to pull herself from her writing for her only granddaughter."

Amelia responded with a hint of desperation in her voice. "Mom, don't worry! Now you better get Dad to the train station and yourself to work."

"You are right about that." Karen hugged her daughter and left the room.

Following her parent's departure, Amelia climbed the stairs to her bedroom. The second floor landing gave view to a sparkling September sun that framed itself within the large foyer window high above the home's front door. In its brightness and seeming perfection, the sun reminded Amelia of her loving family. Though her parents did pretty much the same thing every day, they never seemed to tire of their routine. Both Ken and Karen Morelli were bright people with Ivy League educations from Yale University. Amelia was certain they could have done anything with their lives. Still, ever since she could remember, her dad commuted by train to his downtown Manhattan office where he worked as a legal consultant for Cantor Fitzgerald. While her mom, never without a book, rather appropriately worked as a librarian with the New Haven Library. Amelia wondered if she would ever be as content with her own life, the way in which her parents seemed to be with theirs.

Unaccustomed to wasting time, by 8:00 AM, Amelia was posed in front of her bedroom desk top computer, ready to begin a school assignment. Muffled sounds emanated from the wall TV. At the same time she forced bites of a cereal breakfast bar down, followed by sufficient gulps of milk. "Nasty", she said to herself. Shaking her head she mumbled under her breath. "Now, why am I such a mess over the prospect of sharing my thoughts with Mom and Dad?" How she longed for the anticipated evening conversation to be behind her.

Amelia breathed a deep breath. Once again fighting to regain her composure, she doggedly began to search the internet for information applicable to a social studies project which was due by the end of the week. Soon lost to the task at hand, she began breathing easier. The rosy color returned to the girl's flawless translucent skin. In all but thirty minutes she had scrolled down several pages of suitable material. "Oh, Mr. Jameson, you are going to love this! Right on!"

The girl continued her work, only stopping to dutifully return her dirty milk glass to the kitchen. Upon her return to the bedroom, the corner of her eye caught the sight of a menacing dark cloud seemingly leaping out of the TV screen. Amelia blinked, than stared incredulously at the smoking cigar like shape dominating the center of the screen. Her mind raced to fast forward; could she be looking at the Manhattan twin towers? Could that imploding smoking cigar possibly be the same building where her dad had worked for so many years? Breathless, she struggled to speak. "Oh, please God, this can't be happening?" Frantically, Amelia searched for the TV remote hidden within the array of clutter strewed upon the bed. Unable to locate the remote, she flew out of her room and down the stairs. Immediately she turned on the 52 inch TV her father had recently mounted onto the family room wall.

The TV reporter's face looked grotesquely distorted as he spewed his life changing words. "To repeat, this just came in. You are looking at obviously a very disturbing live shot there.

That is the World Trade Center, and we have unconfirmed reports this morning that a plane has crashed into one of the towers of the World Trade Center. CNN Center right now is just beginning to work on this story, obviously calling our sources and trying to figure out exactly what happened, but clearly something relatively devastating happening this morning there on the south end of Manhattan. That is once again, a picture of one of the towers of the World Trade Center."

Amelia lunged for the telephone. Her hand found the cold receiver as the phone emitted its loud piercing ring. "Mom, is that you?" The pitch of Amelia's voice continued to rise. "Something awful has happened."

Amelia heard her mother's thin though controlled voice. "Yes, I'm looking at it right now! Let's not panic, Dad still may be okay! They still are sketchy as to whether a plane has hit the north or the south building. I'm coming home; stay where you are and try to remain calm. Phone your Granny Lou as soon as I hang up. Bye!"

CHAPTER 2

The Long Wait

Karen made arrangements to leave her work, and against the advice of friends she remained insistent that she drive herself home.

Once alone in the driver's seat of her Camry, her mind began to entertain the endless possibilities as to her husband's fate. She pleaded and whimpered to herself. "Ken you can't leave us now! You have too much to live for. I could never accept losing you now!"

Frozen in the moment, Karen maneuvered her vehicle through the familiar streets of New Haven, Connecticut. She continued to make her unspoken pleas to both her God and her husband. She whispered. "Darling, remember how our families believed we were ill suited for one another. Oh, how we proved them wrong! And then there was Amelia. She is so like you, gifted in so many ways. We all have so much to live for. Ken, wherever you are, please don't die!"

Karen's tears fell hard upon the steering wheel as she pulled into her garage. She patted her face with a Kleenex, wiping the tear drops from her cheeks. "Lord, please keep me strong, I can't let Amelia see me like this. Besides, Ken will be alright, I know you will take care of him." She steadied herself and entered the house.

Amelia called out to her mom. "I am in the den. Hurry, you won't believe what has just happened!" Amelia remained fixated upon the TV, as Karen hurried into the den.

Karen pulled her daughter close to her, and then directed her attention toward the TV. "What is it, what's happened?"

Amelia shrieked. "Look, there is smoke coming from the other building. They think another plane has crashed. Nobody seems to know what is going on. I tried to call Dad on both his office and cell phone but there was no answer. Oh, Mom, I am so scared!"

"I know dear, I am too! I tried to contact your father before I left work, but I couldn't reach him either. Did you call Granny Lou?"

"Yes, she and Granddad are on their way." Amelia's voice cracked. "Oh, why doesn't someone do something and get those people out of there!"

*　　*　　*　　*

Following Amelia's frantic phone call, Lou and Mike McDowell abruptly left their breakfast table, and began the twenty minute drive to their daughter's home.

Robotically, Mike turned on the car radio; all broadcasts were interrupted and there was immediate news about the Manhattan twin towers.

Lou unaccustomed to being in the passenger seat, cautioned her husband. "Mike you better slow down, I don't believe I have ever seen so much traffic this time of the morning. People must be moving around in response to this horrific situation."

"We are okay Lou, just try to calm down. Don't anticipate the worse before it happens."

"I can't help it. I have this hollow feeling in my gut that Ken is gone. Of course, I would never say such a thing to

Karen or Amelia. I do hope they get through this and that I am wrong about Ken."

"No matter what we say or do, let's not rob Karen and Amelia of any hope they maybe hanging onto. I guess the best course of action is to pray our heads off."

"Mike, for once, I am not going to argue with you!"

*   *   *   *

Amelia continued to stare at the TV. While her mother fell into Granny Lou's comforting arms. Even though Amelia's head was spinning and her body felt as though it belonged on a slab, she was determined to remain strong, no matter what the day might bring.

Lou and Mike seated themselves near Amelia on the oversized sofa. All eyes fixated upon the riveting scene unfolding before them. Amelia felt her granddad's arm around her shoulders; the nearness of the three bodies to her own, gave her a modicum of comfort.

As though on cue, the TV ominously bleeped, followed by the broadcaster's announcement that a third plane had just crashed into the Pentagon. Mike muttered under his breath. "This is only getting worse! Has anyone tried to contact Frank and Florence?"

"I have been trying to get them for the past hour, there is no answer at their home and Frank's cell phone is always busy." Karen's face was ashen and her mouth trembled as she spoke.

"Knowing Frank and Florence, they will be actively trying to get information about their son's whereabouts. Okay, honey, let me try to get Frank on his cell; I'll just go into the hall where I can hear better." Mike quickly stepped into the hall and dialed. "Frank is that you? This is Mike. We are here with Karen and Amelia. Is there any news about Ken?"

Frank's voice sounded tight and hoarse. "No, nota yet. Luckily Florence and I spenta the night in our city apartment over the a restauranti. Other the wise we a would nota have a been able to geta into Manhattan. We're just aheaded a down to thea Worlda Trade Center to see ifa we can finda anything out."

"Be careful down there, Frank. Let us know as soon as you find anything out about Ken." Mike kept shaking his head yes, as he listened.

"Tella the girls I will abring Ken home to thema tonight, you willa see!" Frank said goodbye and hung up.

Mike's cell phone clicked, as a blood curdling scream emanated from the den. When he re-entered the room Karen stood pointing at the TV. At the same time she held her opposite hand firmly over her mouth in an attempt to stifle yet another scream. Amelia and Lou remained silent, lost to the cloud of dust and debris mushrooming within the TV screen. Breathless, a live CNN reporter choked out the surreal words. "Oh, this is unbelievable; the South building of the World Trade Center has just collapsed into a pile of smoke and rubble. The carnage is unimaginable, what a sad day this is for us all."

"Get those people out of there; get my dad out of that building!" Amelia's veins showed through her translucent skin.

Lou remained uncommonly mute, only speaking to reassure Amelia. "Child, I'm sure they are doing all they can do to save as many people as possible."

Karen's voice quivered as she hung onto her mother's words. "You are right, Mom. Amelia, they said it was the South Tower that has collapsed. There still may be a chance that Ken could get out. Why, Ken may not even be in the building; I remember one morning his train was delayed and he hadn't arrived at work until 10:00 AM. If anyone can get himself out of a bad situation, it is Ken!"

Momentarily reassured by her mother's words, Amelia and the rest of the family returned to the abyss of their own private despair. Mike turned up the volume on the TV as the reporter spoke his ominous words. "It is estimated that the plane which had crashed into the North Tower, struck the building somewhere between the 93 and the 99 floors. It is very doubtful that anyone in that area of the building would have survived. In the mean time, firefighters and police continue to work feverishly to evacuate the lower floors of the building."

With tear stained faces the family sat mesmerized by the chaos unfolding just miles from their home. Within an hour of the South Tower collapse, the North Tower began its descent, resembling a fragile sand castle, rather than a structure composed of stone and steel. Amelia remained immobilized by the strange sights and sounds played out before her. Only the look of terror upon her mother's normally composed face permeated the numbness which enveloped her.

Karen directed her gaze at her father before bolting from the couch. "Please Dad, I beg you, drive me into Manhattan; I need to learn what has happen to Ken."

As she started toward the door, Mike gently grasped Karen's arm. "Honey, that is not even an option, the city has already been cordoned off to incoming traffic. Any attempt to enter the city would be futile. It is best that we all just wait here for either Ken or Frank to call."

The hours passed without word. The beautiful September sky began to set, oblivious to the shattered lives left to its ensuing darkness. The family fell in and out of exhausted sleep. In fear of missing the non-stop CNN broadcasts, no one left the den except for trips to the bathroom and kitchen. Sandwiches and sliced fruit prepared by Lou, remained untouched.

The following day, at 5:11 AM, the home phone rang. Mike grabbed the receiver. "Hello, hello, I can hardly hear you! Who is this?" With effort Mike finally distinguished the breathless voice of Frank Morelli.

Frank was calling from the couple's restaurant, which had turned into an outpost. Slowly he reported what he and

Florence had learned through one of Ken's co-workers. "Well, it seems that thisa fellow Ken works awith, hada exchanged a words witha him as hea stepped off thea elevator at thea 104ᵗʰ floor. Thata was approximately 8:30 AM. In the mean time thisa same guy gets a ona thea elevator whicha takes him to thea lobby. From a there he leaves thea building and hea hails a cab to a take ahim to an early morning appointment. Within minutes of hisa cab ride thea unthinkable happens." There is a long pause. "Firefighters have a told me that no a one above thea point of impact coulda be rescued." Between sobs, and now barely audible, Frank continued. "Mya beautiful a son is a gone! *Per favore di dire le ragazze.* I a mean a please share a thea horrible news with a Karen and Amelia, I ajust can'ta do it." The receiver clicked and Frank's words resonated in Mike's ear.

Mike continued to clutch the phone receiver, while tears trickled down his ashen checks. Amelia and Karen remained mute, in dread of the words which would follow the thump of the phone receiver. Like lasers their eyes pierced Mike's soul as he gently gathered up Karen in his arms and whispered in her ear. Lou, in response to the inevitable, pulled Amelia close to her. Any attempt to remain strong was lost to profound grief. The family sobbed and held one another tight, their bodies welded together in pain and protest. Mike and Lou put all words of consolation and faith aside and openly grieved with their daughter and granddaughter.

CHAPTER 3

Lives in Continuum

Everything looked just as she had remembered. There were the long lines of school buses with the familiar faces squeezing out of the narrow exit doors. The same deafening chatter prevailed. Amelia felt sorry for the impotent figure wrapped in a yellow harness, feverishly blowing into a tiny whistle in an attempt to keep order. She wondered why nothing at all had changed, while at the same time her own life would never be the same. Feeling no less out of place than a space alien about to be ejected from her mother's Camry, Amelia searched the horizon for a refuge. Desperate for anything which would help her regain a sense of belonging.

Amelia jerked forward as her mother stopped abruptly upon maneuvering the vehicle into the familiar drop off space. "Okay, Amelia, we made it. Are you sure you are up to this, you look a little pale? I don't know if this is such a good idea; Dr. Beale said…"

"Mom, stop. I will be just fine; in fact I see Trish headed in our direction. She said she would meet me in front of the school. Don't worry, I'll see you later. Amelia gave her mother a cursory glance as she brushed her lips gently upon her cheek before bounding from the car.

Together the girls watched as Karen slowly pulled away from her daughter's school. Amelia felt great comfort in the company of her long time friend. Firmly, Trish placed a consoling arm around Amelia's waist. "Oh Melie, I am so sorry about your dad; how is it going? I wanted to talk with you at your dad's service, but my parents hurried me out the door. You are darn near impossible to get a hold of. How is your mom doing?"

"Trish, I am going to give you an adult answer to an adult situation. She is doing as good as can be expected. Now, please, can't we just talk about something else, anything!"

"Oh, I am such a dunderhead! I just wanted to help and all I've done is make you feel worse."

Amelia wistfully looked at her tearful childhood friend. "Oh, Trish, you have not made me feel worse. I doubt if there is anything in this world right now that could, except… Why don't you tell me what I have missed these past few weeks!"

"Oh, you won't believe that Cynthia Ambrose, she is trying to horn her way into……"

"Hi Melie, Trish. It's good to see you back." A boy with downcast eyes rushed by; he looked more awkward than Amelia remembered. His lips were held tightly together, appearing uncertain as to whether he should flash his clown like smile.

"Thanks, Scotty!"

Trish pulled at Amelia's arm. "Listen we had better get a move on it or we will be late for homeroom." Amelia picked up her pace and followed Trish into the building.

*   *   *   *

The cafeteria line seemed longer and slower then Amelia had remembered. The only thing she wanted was to find an obscure table in some corner where she and Trish could just sit and maybe not even say a word. Normally, the two girls would have mingled with the New Haven Junior High *I-Pods*. Though, even on a good day, that was something Amelia could easily do without.

Trish pulled Amelia toward the boisterous group. "Come on Melie, let's sit with the *I-Pods*. They will catch you up on what you have missed these past two weeks."

"No, Trish, you go ahead. I am in no mood for who did who, or even less enthralling who might have had a boob job."

"Why, Amelia Morelli, your mom would be mortified to hear you talking like that."

"You are probably right, Trish; but, leave my mom out of this."

"Oh Melie, I did not mean any disrespect. As moms go, you know I adore your mom. Okay, where would you rather sit; I really didn't want to hear that stuff either."

Amelia shot Trish a weak smile, while stealthily leading her to the far end of the large cafeteria. Only the nerds sat in this isolated area of the room. Here in silent anonymity, Amelia and Trish seated themselves, focusing their attention upon their over-cooked burgers and fries.

Trish's face mirrored her discomfort. "I'm afraid to ask, but how did your morning go?"

Amelia's words were uncharacteristically hard. "Well, why should you be any different? Everyone else in this school acts afraid. They can't even look me in the eye. It feels like everyone in the whole school is juggling a nitroglycerin stick at the end of their nose, terrified that if they say or do the wrong thing, we will all be blown to bits."

"Melie, that's not fair!"

Amelia looked down at her half eaten burger. "You know Trish, you are right and I am truly sorry. Just forget the whole thing. Why don't you finish telling me about, what's her name, Cynthia."

Trish curled her lips. "Oh, that sneaky, red haired, devil."

Amelia, as amused as she had been in weeks, quipped. "Trish, have you forgotten, you have red hair as well"

"That may be so, but I am not a scheming, pig faced, phony."

"I agree, you are not. But what did she do to deserve that distinction?"

"Well, while you were absent from music practice, she darn near convinced Mr. Taylor that she should take over the lead pianist part in the December Christmas Pageant."

"So why didn't Mr. Taylor jump at that?"

Trish looked thoughtful. "Well, my dad says everything is politics. So I'm only guessing now, but I think Mr. Taylor could not wait until our own child prodigy, *cela vous est*, moved from Meadowbrook Elementary to New Haven Jr. High. That makes New Haven Jr. High an almost shoo-in for winning the orchestra intramurals in the spring."

Amelia felt her eyes moisten. "It's funny, my dad use to say that."

Trish looked confused. "Say what?"

"Never, mind. So you think that even though Mr. Taylor is uncertain if I am up to it, he might be afraid of turning me off if he gives Cynthia the lead part in the Christmas Pageant. Am I right?"

"Exactly!"

*   *   *   *

Within minutes the music hall cacophony would be silenced. Amelia, always amazed by the abrupt transformation, sat uncomfortably posed in front of the piano. Trish, with flute pressed lightly against her lips, while other classmates stood motionless behind their assigned instruments, waited in quiet anticipation. With arms raised, Mr. Taylor stood tall upon his platform, looking like a god in total command of his young worshipers.

Amelia wondered if Mr. Taylor could see the beads of sweat seeping from her forehead. She was certain he did, and wondered if she would be able to finesse her way through the practice. Before she took her next breath, his large smooth hands waved methodically in the air, and the room was filled with harmony. Strange as it seemed, she knew she continued to be dragged through the simple piece by the rest of the orchestra.

With each selection it became more difficult for Amelia to maintain her timing. To her great relief, Mr. Taylor ended practice session early. He dismissed the class and discreetly motioned Amelia to his office. Trish trailed behind, sitting just outside of Mr. Taylor's room, well within ear shot of his conversation with Amelia.

*   *   *   *

"Amelia, please have a seat. Well, Amelia, I am so glad to see you back at school. I'm so very sorry about your dad. I hope you know that you have been in the thoughts and prayers of your teachers and fellow students since that terrible day. Please let me know if there is anything I can do to make your return to school any easier."

For a second Amelia sat quietly, somewhat stunned that Mr. Taylor had not chastised her for her poor performance. She thought for a moment, before realizing what she needed to do. "Thank you, Mr. Taylor, actually there is something you can do for me."

"What's that, Amelia?"

"I would like for you to excuse me from orchestra practice for the rest of the semester."

Momentarily speechless, Mr. Taylor's mouth dropped open in obvious disbelief. "Are you sure about that, Amelia? You have worked so hard your entire life, to be able to play the piano the way in which you do. I confess I was looking forward to having such an accomplished pianist in the school orchestra. You would have made my job so much easier."

"Mr. Taylor, you must have noticed the way I flubbed up today, why it was awful. I just can't seem to focus."

Mr. Taylor looked thoughtful. "Well, I confess I noticed your timing was not what it should have been; but, don't you think you are being a little hard on yourself. After all, this is your first day of school since losing you father."

Amelia shook her head. "I'm afraid it is more than that. I really need for you to excuse me from class. No one would question your decision."

"No one, that is, but me. I can't believe you want to do this! But if that is really what you want, I will speak with Mr. Godfrey later today."

Sheepishly, Amelia interjected. "There is one other thing, Mr. Taylor. Would you please give the piano lead in the Christmas pageant to Cynthia Ambrose."

Once again, Mr. Taylor looked stunned. "I don't know which of your requests have surprised me most. Is Cynthia a friend of yours?"

"Not really. I have heard her play a number of times and I think she would do New Haven proud."

"You would as well, Amelia. But, I am not going to force you into something you really don't want to do. I am hopeful you will return to us next semester."

Amelia, while relieved by Mr. Taylor's compliance with her request, at the same time felt a deep emptiness. "Thank you, Mr. Taylor; I will try."

Looking as down trodden as she felt, Amelia quickly left Mr. Taylor's office. Two steps out the door, she found herself nose to nose with Trish. Looking as though steam was venting from her pretty ears, Trish confronted Amelia. "You didn't, how could you give away the lead instrumental part in the

Christmas pageant to Cynthia, of all people. Oh, I think I am going to be sick!"

Tears streaming down her cheeks as she faced her friend, Amelia looked like a wounded animal. "Trish, you have finally succeeded in making me feel worse. You know I see the pity in everyone's eyes, in their voices, yet no one really understands that the girl they knew is gone. She is gone forever. Now, I'm sorry for disappointing everyone, but I just can't do it right now! Let someone else be the star for a change." Without further explanation Amelia bolted down the corridor leaving Trish to ponder her words.

CHAPTER 4

Past Present

Amelia sat twisting the white beaded ponytail clasp she had removed from her lustrous hair. Though she believed Dr. Beale to be a nice enough man, she resented what she viewed, as his attempt to dissect every synapse of her brain. Had her mother not insisted that she continue to meet with the sanguine shrink, she would have stopped many months earlier. Resigned to her fate, she waited for the familiar invitation.

"The Doctor is ready to see you, Amelia." Robotically, Amelia stood up and smiled politely in the direction of the friendly, yet sterile, female voice.

Upon entering Dr. Beale's office, she found him already seated in the shopworn cream colored chair. "Well, young lady, how is your week going?"

"Pretty much the same, school and homework. Not much else." She scrutinized Dr. Beale's facial expression and body language for clues as to how he was processing her deliberately fail-safe response.

Amelia was determined to learn as much about this

fatherly figure's internal workings, as she knew, he was to learn about her own. Though, she suspected, following a full year of therapy, that Dr. Beale was far too practiced a therapist to forfeit any clues that he did not intend for her to have.

"Amelia, you are certainly a dedicated student; I imagine your grades are very good?"

Amelia fidgeted on the cushioned magenta couch. "Mostly A's with a few B's.

"You are to be commended! Now, I know what I am about to ask you to do is not easy, especially for someone as young as yourself; but I am going to ask you to try. I want you to imagine what you believe you will be doing five years from now."

Amelia looked as though she had been hit in the gut with one of Dr. Beale's text books. Her eyes filled with tears and her normally serene face became uncommonly angry over what she interpreted as her mother's betrayal. "Dr. Beale, did my mother suggest that you ask me that question? It's always about playing the piano, isn't it?"

In spite of her unexpected outburst, Dr. Beale responded calmly. "Amelia, I'm glad you asked. Let me assure you that though your mother is also one of my patients, she in no way directs the course of our sessions. What we discuss rests with you alone. Now, is there anything you wanted to share about your piano playing or would you rather spend the time talking about something else?"

Amelia's anger dissipated as quickly as it appeared. She dropped her head, and in a barely audible voice spoke. "While I have survived the first anniversary of my dad's death, I am dreading my planned sixteenth birthday celebration."

"Can you tell me why you are dreading your birthday party?"

Amelia felt her throat muscles tighten, so much so, that she barely recognized the high-pitch whisper which left her mouth. Dr. Beale leaned toward Amelia so he might better hear her response.

With awkwardness, uncommon for her, Amelia continued. "My grand papa and grand mama have arranged for a large gathering of friends and family at their Long Island home, this coming weekend, for my birthday. This is the first real celebration without my dad, and I just do not know if I can handle it."

"Have you spoken to your mother about your feelings concerning the party?"

"No, I did not want to upset her any more than I have already."

"Can you share with me why you believe you have upset your mother?"

"There are a lot of things since my dad died. Dr. Beale, I just want to talk about the party, right now?"

Following her confession, Amelia felt somewhat relieved.

Dr. Beale lifted the photo of his three teenage children from his desk and handed it to Amelia. "Amelia, as you have probably surmised, these are my three kids. Do you know what upsets me more than anything else my children might do?"

Unabashed, Amelia's face lit up, feeling both surprised and curious. Rarely, if ever, had Dr. Beale personalized his sessions with her. As she fingered the photo, she really wanted to know what upset her shrink the most when dealing with his own children. "No, Dr. Beale, I didn't think you ever got upset."

The therapist rolled his eyes. "I am most upset when I suspect that my children do not trust me with their truth. Their truth being what they are feeling about any given situation in their lives."

Amelia and Dr. Beale sat in silence as she reflected upon his words.

Pointing to the clock, Dr. Beale smiled. "You have skillfully managed an unprecedented role reversal, and in that time, our session has come to an end. Amelia, you have a loving and understanding mother, please think over what we have talked about."

*   *   *   *

As she waited to be ushered into Dr. Beale's office, Karen Morelli sat in the same chair her daughter had occupied two days earlier. She thought how strange it was to be sharing her deepest feelings with a virtual stranger. Yet, unlike Amelia, the fragile woman recognized that she needed help in peeling away the layers of hurt and pain which had enveloped her since her husband's death. She realized, that within the year she had been in counseling, so much of what she had discussed with Dr. Beale, centered upon her daughter rather than her life with Ken. She envisioned Amelia's lovely face, the thickly lashed eyes set within a cherubic face. She could only claim her daughter's green eyes and delicate features, otherwise the girl so reminded her of Ken. Blessed in many ways, Amelia had inherited her father's same intelligence and proclivity for music. How it hurt Karen to watch Amelia throw away her talent.

"Mrs. Morelli. Mrs. Morelli, are you okay? Dr. Beale will see you now."

Karen looked up in surprise. "Oh, yes, I'm sorry I must have been lost to my thoughts."

The therapist greeted Karen with his usual warm smile. "And how are you today, Karen?"

Willingly, Karen began. "Dr. Beale, I confess I am at a loss. Slowly, though steadily, I believe I am finding my way through this journey with grief. Even if there are still times when I slip back into that sleepless despair I had experienced the first few months following Ken's death, there are more moments when I am momentarily able to leave my pain behind. Usually, with both pride and guilt, I accomplish this while reading a new book and sipping a steaming cup of tea."

With usual candor, Dr. Beale spoke. "Well, this is all good my dear, so can you tell me what is troubling you?"

Chest fallen, and tears welling up in her eyes, Karen hesitantly, continued. "Well, though I seem to know exactly where I am with my journey, my girl remains a puzzle. I never know where she is with this same struggle. Even the controlled Karen Morelli, from time to time breaks the silence and screams at the world. At the same time, Amelia remains mute and withdrawn, even in response to my own uncharacteristic outbursts."

Gently, Dr. Beale spoke. "Karen, it is true that both you and Amelia share grief over the loss of a husband and father. Yet, no struggle is the same; individuals deal with grief in their own way and in their own time. So try to describe for me what you have observed in respect to her behavior."

"Well, over this past year, though Amelia has never breached any rules nor given anyone cause for anger, she has lost her joy for living. A love for life had always been a part of her nature. Now, she no longer sees her friends and refuses to participate in so many of the things she once did. I'm especially concerned that she no longer plays her piano. Everyone has noticed the change in her since her dad's death. I do not know how to help her!" Karen openly wept.

Dr. Beale remained silent, until Karen regained her composure. After she wiped her eyes, he spoke. "Karen, can you review for me why Amelia's piano playing is of such significance for you?"

With astonishment, Karen blurted out what she considered to be the obvious. "Well, we talked about this when Amelia and I first began therapy. My daughter is a musical prodigy, and the plan was for her to attend the Manhattan Julliard School of Music. Why, she has been playing the piano since she was three years old."

"Yes, yes, of course Karen you have told me this, but what

was her relationship to the piano. Was the discipline imposed upon her, how did she become a, let us say, a player?"

Karen moved back to a happier time. "It seems like yesterday when Ken first placed our two years old daughter upon his lap as he exercised the Morelli's old white Steinway piano. It was then that the love triangle began. Ken's face beamed with pride, when Amelia remained amused for an inordinate period of time. Soon after, our toddler begged to be perched in front of the piano. She would point her small finger at the imposing instrument and in a clear, imploring voice she would say, Dada, me play!"

Karen smiled to herself. "Of course, at first she produced less than harmonic sounds, though Ken never noticed. It was not long before she began to bang out notes that belonged together."

Dr. Beale posed his next questioned. "Is that when she began taking piano lessons?"

"Yes, Amelia was all but three years old when Mrs. Nina Corning began giving her lessons. Ken would sit in on her practice sessions whenever he could. Did I mention earlier, that together, Amelia and Ken had learned to read music? Before those lessons, Ken had played by ear."

Uncommon curiosity eclipsed Dr. Beale's face. "I would have thought that Ken had known how to read music before those lessons."

"Yes, I was surprised as well. But it seems that despite Ken's musical genius, his parents always pushed him in other directions. They found music acceptable as a hobby, though not the main focus of their son's education. So, as a child he was self-taught, viewing the piano as a source of fun. As he grew older it became a diversion from the strong concentration of business, soon to be imposed upon him."

Dr. Beale stroked his smooth shaven chin. "So the piano has always been a big part of Amelia's life?"

"Oh, yes, at an early age she shared her dad's delight in

the instrument and she became accustomed to long hours of practice. The love and enthusiasm Amelia had for playing the piano was very much intertwined with the love she had always had for her dad. After his death, I expected that she would have retreated to the piano for solace, instead days go by without so much as an hour spent in practice. Everyone close to Amelia fears that her dream of studying at Julliard will die for her just as her dad has." Tears trickled down Karen's face. "I simply do not know how to help!"

Dr. Beale warmly reached for Karen's hand. "I can assure you that what you are witnessing might have occurred even under the best of circumstances. Amelia is an adolescent, dealing with not only the world of an adolescent, but also the loss of a beloved parent. At this time I do not believe medication is warranted, as I would not describe her sadness as clinical depression. My advice is to keep her as involved as possible with school and anything else she might express an interest in. Be patient with her, and continue to show your love and support. I believe you both will come through this."

Karen thanked Dr. Beale. Reassured, though unconvinced, Karen remained unnerved by the thought she might be losing her daughter as surely as she had lost Ken.

CHAPTER 5

The Birthday Party

"I can't believe you will be sweet sixteen in all but four days." Karen appeared to search her daughter's face for a trace of its old exuberance.

Amelia immediately looked away, determined to avoid her mother's questioning green eyes. "Oh Mom, that is such an archaic cliché! Most of the sixteen year old girls, I know, are anything but sweet."

"Well, I was not referring to most sixteen year old girls. I do hope you can muster up a little more enthusiasm for the extravaganza that your grand mama and grand papa have planned for you! Honestly, Amelia, you can be very trying at times."

Karen's drawn face stabbed at Amelia's conscience. At the same time Dr. Beale's last words to her, echoed within her head. In an instant, Amelia's detached demeanor vanished, and she spouted out her protest. "I don't want to go to the party! Who wants to be paraded about, like some sort of little orphan Annie?"

Karen's lip began to tremble. "Oh, Amelia, you know how

very much your grandparents love you and that they would never do anything to hurt you. They have been planning this for months, you can't disappoint them. I only wish you would have said something sooner; is it because this will be the first celebration without Dad? Of course it is. Oh, honey, I do understand!"

Her mother's escalating distress was more than Amelia could bear, and she immediately recanted. "Yes, Mom, you are right about everything. I will try very hard to get through the day, I promise."

*　　*　　*　　*

Amelia's birthday brought with it no shortage of sunshine. Rays of light shone through the French doors of the Morelli living room. Beyond the French doors was a massive sun room that featured a kaleidoscopic view of the gardens below. In these same gardens Karen and Ken Morelli had exchanged marriage vows eighteen years earlier. Since then, nothing had visibly changed on the Long Island estate, save the delicate hues of spring were now replaced by a palette of fall colors. Seductively the living tapestry of yellow and red leaves clung to the trees, allowing for only glimpses of the mercurial Long Island Sound.

The Morelli guest list was long, with many of the same relatives and friends who over the years had attended other family gala parties. Those in attendance today, knew that this event held its own uniqueness. Though a celebration of Amelia's sixteenth birthday, this would be the first grand party without the presence of Ken Morelli. Appropriately, people wore their party faces. Adorned in stylish clothes, men and women participated in the expected banter. Yet, no degree of glitter or clever conversation could mask an air of awkward resolve not to ruin the party with a misspoken word or related remembrance.

Inevitably, the reticence to make reference to the tragedy

would be tossed aside. A statuesque brunette in a yellow fitted satin dress gleefully alerted those around her that the party girl had arrived. "Oh, here she comes! My word she looks stunning, who would ever think she had suffered such a loss. And Karen, a little thinner but none the worse for wear. What brave women!"

An older woman added. "Well it has been over a year, young people seem to get over these things better than we old folks. Don't you think? Oh, I love that emerald green tunic pants suit Amelia is wearing. It plays so deliciously off of her green eyes and that long straight dark hair. She is such a beauty!"

*   *   *   *

Amelia took a long, deep breath before entering the massive living room. She held her head high as though she were stepping upon a stage to perform at a recital. Gracefully, she moved her tall delicate body through the seventy-five well wishers. Only once did she turn her head back to see if her entourage followed behind her. With relief, she caught a glimpse of her mother, and Mike and Lou McDowell, not far in her wake.

Despite the smiles and polite hellos uttered by Karen and the McDowells, only Amelia successfully masked the uncertainty of the moment. While poised beyond her years, Amelia silently prayed for a miracle which would release her from the charade she felt forced to participate in. To her great satisfaction, that miracle came swiftly by way of her three younger cousins.

The exuberant greeting of the three vivacious children momentarily fractured the tension percolating within the room. Drew Morelli, age ten and the youngest of the three children, wrapped his stocky arms around Amelia's waist. "Oh, Melie, I have missed you so much! Come with me to Pony's Place!" Tim and Lilly Tucker joined in and together the three shuffled the willing teenager to the stairs. Down they went to an area of the house, that over the years, the children had claimed as their own. Today more than ever, the room served as a respite from the well wishers upstairs.

Below the oversized sun room where many of the guests now congregated, was Pony's Place. The room had been named in honor of the Morelli's massive Newfoundland Retriever, whom the children, affectionately called Pony. Like Pony, the room was large. Its contents included two comfortable sofas and complementary armchairs, tastefully placed upon a gold and black mosaic-tile floor. There were other attractions in the room, including a television/DVD player hidden in an ornate oriental cabinet. Adjacent to the cabinet was an old fashion soda fountain that had been moved from the downtown restaurant. Strategically placed behind the fountain was a refrigerator encased by rows of shelves piled high with treats befitting Pony and visiting grandchildren. Not to be overlooked, was the family's vintage white Steinway piano. The piano had been unobtrusively placed within the far corner of the room adjacent to the servant's quarters. Atop the piano were placed several family photos. A gold-frame held a portrait of Ken with his small daughter upon his lap, as he played the white piano.

The children babbled amongst themselves, while Amelia sat quietly observing them as she had seldom done before. Drew most resembled her Uncle Joe and Frank Morelli, while the Tucker children were fair and tall, more like her father's sister Sheila and his mother.

Drew's dark eyes shined as he impishly questioned Amelia. "Melie, are the big guys coming to your party?"

"No, Drew. You know that Matt and Andy are away at college. In fact Aunt Pat and Uncle Alex are in Vermont right now visiting with Andy." The McDowells were glad that Alex and Pat McDowell had opted to celebrate Amelia's birthday a week earlier. The family believed that fewer relatives at today's celebration might be less stressful for Karen and Amelia.

Drew's face showed his obvious disappointment. "Oh, but I was going to arm wrestle Andy to his knees!" Lilly and Tim rolled their eyes and smiled, while Amelia gently consoled her young cousin. Though good-natured children, Tim and Lily often responded with impatience toward Drew's antics. Amelia, on the other hand, enjoyed the young boy; she always knew when and how to rein him in.

The four cousins continued to snuggle within the embrace of the cushioned sofa. Drew impulsively wrapped his arms about Amelia. "Pony and I will protect you, Melie, and never let anyone hurt you, ever!" Drew hopped from the couch and corralled a less than willing, Pony. Exerting all his strength, he dragged the large canine to the rest atop Amelia's ill prepared feet. Surprised at Drew's fervent show of affection and protectiveness, the children sat speechless. Amelia bent down and kissed Drew on his forehead. Following a considerable struggle to remove Pony from her feet, she walked quickly away from her cousins. She did not want them to see the tears welling up in her eyes. In her hast, she found herself standing over the white piano, in the very corner of the room she most wanted to avoid. Unnerved, she gently brushed her fingers through the keyboard, teasing the instrument as she anxiously hurried by. Her cousins remained silent, watching with baited breath as she flirted with the old relic. Amelia knew how much the children enjoyed her playing their irregular requests. She wished she could be lighthearted once again and play for them. Following her father's death, she imagined her family in a huddle, strategically devising a plan to magically transform her back to her old self. Surely, she thought, her cousins would have heard their parent's whispers, and knew of her reluctance to play the piano.

The children remained inordinately silent, and Amelia knew her attempt to hide her discomfort had failed. Finally,

Tim broke the silence. "Let's go down to the shore and do some shell hunting, come on Lilly!" The boy grabbed his sister's arm, while Pony excitedly wagged his tail in favor of the suggestion.

Drew shrieked. "But we will ruin our clothes!" Amelia and the other children knew full well that Drew would not normally give thought to such a trivial concern. It was clear, that prior to attending the party, Drew had been sternly warned against this activity, by their Aunt Sheila. In deference to their aunt, as well as their own parents, the children's unanimous decision was to change into their play cloths. Together, they rushed to the hall closet where their ready to wear denim, hung in wait.

The boys quickly made their way into the adjacent bathroom. They had no intention of waiting on the girls, while they primped themselves for the excursion. Once the boys vacated the room, the girls were left to undress and catch up on current events. Lilly dominated the conversation, and chattered incessantly about her latest crush. "Amelia, I am really in love with Grouper!"

Amelia tried to look serious. "Is that the same Grouper who is the lead singer for the Goldfish Rock band?

Lilly gushed. "One and the same!"

"How can you be in love with someone you have never met?" Amelia gently quizzed.

"Oh, but I did meet him at last Saturday's concert in Manhattan!" Lilly frowned. "Well, we did not exactly meet, but I managed to get up close, and he signed my program. See, I brought it with me!"

Amelia examined the girl's program. "Well, Mom has always warned me that long distant relationships never work. Yet, I'm sure you feel strongly for Grouper, and I am glad for you." Secretly, Amelia took refuge in Lilly's chosen conversation, preferring to focus upon the girl's adolescent fantasies rather than her own raw emotions.

*　　*　　*　　*

While the children played at the shore, Florence and Frank Morelli entertained their guests as only they could. Plans were underway to surprise Amelia with a lustrous black Baby Grand piano. Florence directed any guest willing to help. "Pleasea, everyone justa position yourselves in front of thea piano; when Amelia enters thea room, I willa give you thea cue to a step aside."

Quickly, she moved on to inspect the sumptuous buffet just adjacent to the piano. In the center of the table was a triple tiered chocolate birthday cake, reading *Happy Birthday Amelia, We Love You.* Next to the cake was an elegant vase filled with two dozen yellow long stemmed roses, Amelia's favorites.

Frank and Florence had been relentless in their insistence that Amelia would once again play the piano upon receiving the magnificent new instrument. Mike McDowell's misgivings had not ebbed since learning about the Morelli's plan to present Amelia with the piano in a public display. Only Lou had been able to quell his protests by insisting that they could not put Amelia in a china cabinet for the rest of her life. Finally with bruised ego in check, Mike joined friends and family in helping to prepare for the instrument's unveiling.

*　　*　　*　　*

Mike caught Lou's eye and winked. "Well, who could imagine a more grandiose display in celebration of a sixteenth birthday?"

Lou squeezed her husband's hand. "Don't worry, Mike, it will be alright! Why don't you go and fetch the youngsters from wherever they might have wondered off to."

"Good idea, I need to stretch these long legs of mine." Mike headed for the stairs that led to Pony's Place. A guest redirected him to the gardens, as he had seen the foursome heading down to the shore. Mike walked through the meticulously manicured gardens to the steep stone steps, which lead to the beach. With each step his mood sank, and his fear for his granddaughter intensified. At the very least, he believed she would be embarrassed by her grandparent's ostentatious gift. He felt a twinge of anger toward Lou, for going along with the party plans and the well-intentioned piano. He believed that Lou, of all people, always so in tune with her family, should have known better. As quickly as the thought crossed his mind, Mike chastised himself for blaming her. He muttered to himself. "When a Morelli decides they are going to act upon something, not even persuasive Lou is a match." His thoughts continued. As for Karen, she was but a shade less vulnerable than Amelia. Upon navigating the last step, he shook his head in resignation. "Well, there is no turning back now. Please, God, help Amelia get through this!"

CHAPTER 6

Gifts of Love

In the distance Mike could see the children frolicking at the water's edge. Tim, with Pony in stride, led the beachcombers as they looked for eye-catching shells and rocks. Pony's bark alerted the youngsters that Mike was approaching and that play would have to come to an end. Drew handed his few precious shells to Amelia and ran to meet Mike. In short order, Pony and the other deserters reluctantly followed and headed in Mike's direction.

Mike looked at the seasoned beachcombers and laughed at the sandy lot. "This is not what your mothers had in mind guys; though you are fine by my book. You had better get cleaned up before going up to the dining area." Moans and groans were to no avail, and the group eventually acquiesced to Mike's gentle persuasion.

Within twenty minutes of Mike's instruction, the children cleaned up and ascended the stairs to the living room. Looking scrubbed and robust after their jaunt to the shore, only Drew had telltale signs of the excursion. Having been missed by the girls' inspection, Drew's hasty cleanup had left remnants of blown sand in the center of his forehead. Drew's mother seemed the only one to notice, as the focus of attention was directed at Amelia.

"Ah, here a comes thea beautiful a birthday girl!" Frank announced loudly in his broken English, while guests applauded. Amelia glowed from the past hour of outdoor activity. Her flush face accented her dark hair and green eyes. Graciously she accepted the birthday congratulations from family and friends. Amelia appeared as though the only change in her life had been the passing of yet another year.

As Amelia approached the main table, on cue, guests moved from their position in front of the baby grand piano. Once again, Frank's voice bellowed. "Wella, how do you alike your birthday agift, mya dear one?" Before Amelia could answer, her grand papa enfolded her within the traditional Morelli hug. With champagne glass in hand he flamboyantly continued. "Thisa precious young lady is thea first a rose presented to me and mya lovely wife Florence, by thea eldest of our three a children. Florence and I live a for each of our four grandchildren; since their abirth they have filled our hearts witha pride and joy."

Frank dared to touch upon what the rest of the family had been feeling but were afraid to mention for fear of spoiling the party. "I a wanta toast oura beloved son, taken from us so abruptly and savagely a little morea than a year ago. To a Ken, whom I knowa continues to watch over his a beautiful family. May a the saints watcha over them all!" Tears filled Frank's eyes and he threw a kiss to Karen. Then he kissed his granddaughter upon her forehead, not having to stoop as the two were head to head.

*　　*　　*　　*

Amelia stood silently beside her grand papa, only moving to return his embrace and kiss. Then dry eyed, without a word, she moved and sat erect at the new piano. As though in a trance she began to play *Pachelbel Cannon D,* one of her father's favorite classical pieces. As though on automatic pilot, Amelia did not miss a note. Her grand papa's words reverberated in her head, with the same impact as that of a crescendo. She remained oblivious to the tears which were shed as she continued to play. Midway through the piece, the overwhelming urge to flee finally had its way with her. Before her fingers connected with the waiting keys, she floated far from the stranglehold of pain and guilt, which had enveloped her since her father's death.

When Amelia opened her eyes, she was surprised to find her head cushioned within her grand mama's goose down pillow. She felt a cool damp cloth on her forehead. Slowly she focused upon the faces of her mother and both her grandmothers, hovering over her. "Mom, why am I in Grand Mama's bed? What happened?

Karen embraced her daughter. "Darling, just rest and you will be fine."

"But what happened? One minute I was playing *Pachelbel,* and then everything went blank."

Lou and Florence moved closer to their granddaughter. Lou spoke first, "Amelia you blacked out, fortunately your Uncle Joe caught you before you fell off of the piano bench."

Karen now with tears in her eyes, interjected. "I should have known this might be too much for you, I'm so sorry!"

"Mom, I'm alright. I guess I just did too much on an empty stomach. Please don't cry!"

While Lou tried to comfort Karen, Florence hurried away to prepare a tray for Amelia from the buffet.

*   *   *   *

After nibbling upon the food her grand mama brought to her, Amelia insisted upon returning to the living room and thanking her well wishers for attending the party. No longer the self assured performer who had glided into their midst earlier in the day, Amelia sedately expressed her thanks. "I just wanted to thank everyone for celebrating with me and my family, today. I guess I didn't listen to my mom, and tried to do too much on an empty stomach. You know the rest. I hope I did not spoil your time."

Amelia heard a faint clap that soon erupted into thunder.

Frank waved his arms wildly, and in his baritone voice bellowed above the clapping. *"La mia bella bambina,* we a were all a so worried abouta you." He pointed in the direction of the piano. "Now justa look at what all these a generous people havea brought you!"

Amelia's eyes followed her grand papa's finger to the two feet high pile of brightly wrapped gifts, placed beneath the piano.

Her grand mama reassured Amelia. "Now no a one expects ayou to open all those a gifts today, you a can takea your time witha that. Justa sit quiet Amelia and let us enjoy your a company."

Still feeling light headed, Amelia was grateful that her grand mama had excused her from having to immediately unwrap the enormity of gifts left for her. She weakly smiled. "Thank you so very much!"

Amelia realized that her fatigue was sorely apparent to everyone. Soon after her reappearance, most of the well wishers began to take their leave. Only Stew Dempsey awkwardly lingered behind. With an impressive resume, including an earlier calling to the Jesuit priesthood, he later found himself teaching law at Yale. During his time at Yale, he developed a close friendship with Ken and the Morelli family. Now, seventy-two years of age, his health continued to deteriorate as a result of long-term complications from emphysema. Amelia could not remember seeing him without a cigarette in his hand. Nevertheless, she found it easy to overlook her Uncle Stew's tobacco odor and stained teeth, in light of his affable nature and quick wit.

Sheepishly, Stew approached Amelia. "Ms. Amelia," he playfully addressed her as such, since her early childhood. "I have something for you! If you do not feel up to opening it I will just leave it with you. I didn't think it wise to leave it with the other gifts as it might get lost amongst the larger packages."

"Oh, I think I can manage opening this little box. How very thoughtful, Uncle Stew."

Efficiently, Amelia peeled away the wrapping paper and peered into the opened box. Inside, she found a masculine crucifix of tarnished silver, hanging from a silver chain. Though she was profoundly puzzled, Amelia did not forget her manners. "Thank you so much, Uncle Stew!"

"No, no, you don't understand! Turn the cross over and read the engraved inscription." Stew patiently waited.

Amelia read aloud. "*To Professor Stew Dempsey , May fructus nunquam cado recdentia ex nemus. Your Humble Protégé, in Life and the Law, Kenneth F. Morelli.*"

"Very good, now do you know what that means?" The man's mouth curved into a faint smile.

Now intrigued, Amelia responded. "I know it is Latin, but I do not know its meaning."

"The closest English translation is, *May the fruit never fall far from the tree.*" The aging man looked hard at Amelia for her understanding.

"Uncle Stew, don't you mean, *The fruit never falls far from the tree?*"

"Well, you might say this is the proverbial optimist's play on words, or rather your father's response to the human condition. It is a wish that none of us should ever fall far from our Maker's grace, and likewise from the grace shown us by those we most admire."

"So this is a tribute to you, isn't it Uncle Stew? It's how my dad felt about you, his teacher and friend! Then, why are you giving this to me?"

"This is a tangible reminder of what a good man your father has been. I believe he would like for you to have it. You see, Ms. Amelia, in my eyes your good father never did fall far from the tree, and I do not believe you shall either. Besides, there is no one I would rather give this to." As he spoke he looked older than his years, though Amelia only saw the twinkling blue eyes as he winked at her.

CHAPTER 7
A Helping Hand

Lou wrestled with her bed covers trying to escape the relentless sunlight shining directly into her eyes. In resignation, she sat straight up in bed and grumbled to herself. "That's what I get for doing a lousy job closing the bedroom draw drapes last evening." With a tinge of envy, she gave Mike a quick glance, while he made the soft breathing sounds of sleep. Then she reluctantly pulled herself out of bed.

Following yesterday's gala birthday party, she and Mike had driven Karen and Amelia back to Connecticut. Little of substance was discussed during the ride home. They reviewed the party's grandeur, the unsolicited gifts, and lastly Mrs. Augustine's low-cut dress. Recalling the conversation, Lou mischievously chuckled as she made her way to the bathroom.

Though, her granddaughter had obvious difficulty dealing with the day's festivities, Lou felt a strange sense of relief. Now, all she had to do was convince Mike that things had actually worked out to Amelia's benefit. Deliberately, she rattled the contents of her cosmetic draw so as to arouse her sleeping husband.

It was not long before she heard Mike's playful yell. "Where is my breakfast, woman?"

With good humor, Lou returned the challenge. "Get your sorry buns down stairs and make your own breakfast! Also, I'll have two over easy, if you please."

Before attempting a shower and shave, Mike poked his head into the bathroom to assess his wife's progress. Lou met her husband's appearance with the usual refrain. "Just barge right in, why don't you! I'm about through anyway."

Mike sat on the side of the tub before beginning what the couple over the years had dubbed the *Bathroom Review.* "Well, this time, my dear wife, you had it all wrong. If I did not love you so much I would give you a good tongue lashing."

Lou frowned. "Wait just one minute; I never said it would be easy for Amelia or Karen. But I do believe it may very well have been one of many necessary tiny steps toward healing."

Mike, looking incredulous, shook his head. "You've lost me!"

Look, honey, I'm no psychologist, but no one can bottle up their emotions indefinitely without dire consequence.

Mike doggedly quizzed Lou. "So you believe that fainting, and then nearly breaking your neck by falling off of a piano bench is going to help matters?"

Lou did not mince words in defending her position. "Of course not, but breaking through that self composed façade, will. Though, I have cautioned Karen to go easy on our granddaughter, I am going to be frank with you. There is something very wrong when a young girl gives up school activities, friends, and the focus of her life for the past thirteen years."

"Oh, we are back to her not wanting to play the piano. Maybe she has just decided she wants to do something else with her life."

"Mike, I wish I believed it was just that simple! I think her avoidance of the piano is nothing more than a symptom of what is really bothering our Amelia. I believe there is a lot more behind the changes we have all seen in her, other than merely adolescent fickleness."

"Okay, Lou, you have made your point. I know you have never been one to give up on a family problem. So, I suspect those active brain cells of yours have already concocted a plan."

"Well, as a matter of fact, I have been thinking! Just maybe, Amelia would do well if she got away from everything she has been a part of her entire life; if not physically, than mentally." Lou quickly qualified her statement. "Of course, I'm suggesting just over a short period of time."

Mike shook his head. "Do you mean even away from Karen?"

With defiance Lou replied. "Yes, even her mother. It might do them both some good. I have been entertaining possibly inviting Amelia to assist me with a genealogy search. Something I have planned in preparation for a new book. We could start the research right here at home; then who knows where our search might take us!"

In obvious discomfort, Mike curled his long legs under him in an attempt to maintain his balance on the edge of the bathroom tub. "This genealogy search you are proposing, will it result in a how to do it type of book or are you planning to focus upon an actual family?"

Lou smiled. "Well both, of course! Do you remember when Amelia was about nine or ten, and how she became very interested in her family background? I do believe her interest had been spawned by a visit with Morelli relatives living in Italy. Eventually, her curiosity focused upon whom she might have been named for on the Thomas side of the family. Funny, but the name Amelia isn't Celtic in origin.

"Well, yes, I recall Amelia's fleeting interest in her name

and its family origin. But do you expect a depressed sixteen-year old to jump at the chance to spend weeks with her grandmother; no matter how delightful that said grandmother may be? Mindful, that the sole purpose of time spent would be the pursuit of a bunch of dead relatives, who chances are, lived very ordinary lives?' Mike politely added. "No offense intended!"

"Have you finished? You may be correct, or maybe not. I'll just have to ask Amelia, if she is interested in working with her eccentric Granny Lou in order to find out just how dull the Thomas clan might be."

Mike frowned. "What do you mean the Thomas clan; what about the McDowells, or for that matter, the Morelli side of the family?"

Frustration written on her face, Lou responded. "Well, I just explained that the name Amelia was used on my side of the family. I believe that is what will personalize the search for her. Later, if she so chooses, we can move to other branches of the family. We will see how it goes!"

Mike grinned. "Well don't get touchy! Just let me know when this search sets you a sail for the far corners of the world. I might even help you pack your bags!"

Lou ignored Mike's attempt at humor. "Well, we certainly won't be going anywhere right now. For that matter, we may never leave our own backyard. It depends on what we learn about the family history. I think the best place to start would be upstairs in our cluttered attic. But first, I must talk over my idea with Karen and Amelia, the sooner the better."

"Well, good luck, my dear." Rubbing his stomach, Mike added. "In the meantime, what do you say to breakfast?"

CHAPTER 8

The Attic

Lou watched her granddaughter rummage through the clutter of memorabilia within her attic. The McDowells had occupied the Old Victorian home since their children had been born. Over the years much of the Thomas and McDowell family's history had been boxed, stored and laid to rest within the 900 square foot attic. Items left within its confines were not limited to the immediate family castaways but included those from the extended family, as well.

Amelia looked at her reflection within an ornate, nineteenth century, dress mirror standing against an unfinished wall. After rescuing rhinestone rimmed theatre glasses from an old steamer trunk, Amelia fastidiously placed them upon the bridge of her nose. Her green eyes widened as she gazed at the curious figure wearing the gaudy glasses and an oversized masculine cross. Rather abruptly, she turned her attention away from her mirrored image and questioned her grandmother. "Granny Lou, what exactly should I be looking for up here?"

"Well, as I have explained, we are doing a genealogy search of the Thomas side of the family. Pull out any old photos, books, or documents you believe might be relevant and place them in the middle of the floor. We will go through them later."

Amelia grimaced. "I guess the McDowell and the Morelli side of the family are out of the picture."

Lou laughed. "Now you sound like your granddad. Remember we are researching the use of Amelia as a long-standing, Thomas family name."

"Granny Lou, can I ask you another question?"

"Of course, Amelia, you know you can ask me just about anything. What is it?"

Amelia hesitated. "Well, I was wondering why you were the only one in the family, who approved of Mom and Dad's marriage?"

Lou looked surprised. "Haven't you questioned your mom about that?"

"Of course I have, many times, but she always says that it is no longer very important." In frustration, Amelia shook her head. "Oh, never mind!"

"No, Amelia, you have a right to know. Let me just say it was not so much a case of approving of either your mom or dad; anyone with a brain in their head could see they were both very special young people. Still, because of family differences, there was concern as to whether they were suited for one another as life partners."

Amelia probed further. "Oh, you mean the religious difference, right?"

Well, certainly that was a large part of it, but there was also personality and cultural differences. What a mix, the Calvinistic McDowells, with their long-standing Scotch Irish roots in this country, and the flamboyant, first generation Italian, Morelli family. There was no doubt we had a lot to learn from one another."

"So, how did you know it was going to work, Granny Lou?"

Lou smiled. "Well, I had a wonderful advantage over

everyone else. I was Karen's mother, and I knew her better than anyone, save her Maker."

Amelia nudged her grandmother along. "So what did you know about Mom?"

"I knew that despite your mom's cool and quiet reserve, that she had a deep capacity for love and passion. I also knew, that once, your handsome and charismatic father had taken note of how the light illuminated my girl's pale straight blond hair and shy green eyes, he would be her love forever. And, so it was, that following the couple's meeting at Yale, they would become a campus item for the next two years of their schooling. Despite their short-sighted families, they married and lived happily ever…" Before finishing her sentence, Lou shot a glance in Amelia's direction.

Staring into space, Amelia revisited her sense of helplessness against those malevolent forces which had taken her father's life. "I guess happily ever after only happens in story books! Thank you for answering my question."

"Well, you're welcome. Now, shall we get back to our riveting mission? You know the best place to learn about your ancestors is in your own home. Especially revealing are old pictures, letters and the family bible. Why don't you continue with that old steamer trunk, which has already given up those sophisticated theatre glasses. I'll continue exploring this old armoire."

Four hours into the search, the attic floor lay carpeted with a collage of old photos and family documents. Tired, though determined, Amelia worked diligently in her efforts to open the rusted latch of a smaller and rather unsightly paisley chest.

Out of the corner of her eye, Lou noticed her granddaughter struggling. "Careful, Amelia, don't cut yourself on that old rusted latch. Let me try and pry it open with this screwdriver." Within seconds, Lou was at Amelia's side working the screwdriver in an attempt to release the lock's hold on the old chest.

Amelia watched her grandmother work the old lock. "This reminds me of one of those gothic mysteries where the answer to the riddle lies buried in the contents of an old chest."

"You never know; truth and fiction often mirror one another. There it goes, let's see if there are any secrets in here, shall we?" Expectantly, Lou opened the lid of the battered old chest. Immediately a dank musty odor permeated the air. Lou and Amelia held their breath, turning their faces away from the unpleasant odor. Lou quipped. "Obviously, not my most favorite perfume!"

The offensive odor proved no match for the feisty woman's determination. In no time, Lou began to rummage through the chest's contents. She did so with efficiency and great care, trying not to compromise the items which she handled. "No doubt these are two fine nineteenth century lady's dresses, and beneath them two plainer plaid work dresses. Oh, here, one of the work dresses has been embroidered with the initials M.W. on the left breast pocket."

"Granny Lou, I think we might want to put on gloves before exploring this pile of rags any further."

"Don't tell me my granddaughter is afraid to get her hands dirty?" Undaunted, Lou continued to examine the contents of the old chest, as well as its exterior. "I think that with this magnifying glass, I can just about make out the letters ACG on the rusted chest latch. Now, let us go inside again, and see what we have in these pockets!" Lou smiled broadly, as she pulled out a very fragile, though intact, prayer book.

Amelia moved closer to her grandmother, so she might get a better look. "Be careful Granny Lou, it appears as though the only thing holding the pages together is that equally worn brown leather binder."

"I'll be as careful as possible." Lou gingerly thumbed through the yellowed parchment.

"Look, on the insert of the cover, appears the date February 9, 1854. Granny Lou, with your magnifying glass can you make out the inscription which follows?"

"Yes, my dear, I can. It reads: *To my beloved daughter, Amelia Currick Gale. May this prayer book serve you in times of happiness, as well as in sorrow! Love always, your mother, Adelaide Gale.* I do believe we are on to something! Most old prayer books provide space in the back for names and notations." Lou quickly skipped to the back of the book. "Just as I suspected, there are legible notes on the last few pages. Amelia, use my magnifying glass and your young eyes to read what it says!"

Amelia, squinted as she read the faded print aloud. "Looks like, Mazzie Winfield, followed by Four Corners, Richmond, Virginia. Beneath which is the notation November 28, 1860, 11:00 PM."

"Amelia, this is becoming most fascinating! I have virtually no idea as to how this old chest came to rest in my attic. I am certain that over the years no one has taken the time to examine its contents. Why, I would surmise that at the very least, we have uncovered a wealth of family history in this little chest."

Less animated than her grandmother, Amelia responded. "Well, I guess it is likely that Amelia Currick Gale is a Thomas ancestor. How else would her chest find its way into your attic?"

"That certainly would be a logical foregone conclusion. To think, we may have identified an ancestor who lived during one of the most turbulent times in American history. Our earlier finds certainly pale in comparison with this!"

As hard as she might resist, Amelia began to find her grandmother's escalating excitement contagious. "Do you mean the Civil War, Granny Lou?"

Lou dropped her head. "Yes, it seems like the wars and the killing follow us down through the generations."

Amelia knew only too well the truth behind her grandmother's words. Following a brief remembrance of 9/11, she rallied her defenses and ignored her pain. "Well, Granny Lou, what next? What do we do with, Amelia Currick Gale, and the other bits and pieces of information we have collected?"

Lou methodically reviewed the steps they would take to further the search. "First we will place those family names known to us, into one of the recommended genealogy websites. We will build upon the information we already have. By taking this approach we will work our way down through the generations. Since we are focusing upon ancestors with the name Amelia, our search will be less complicated than it would if we did a more inclusive family study."

Amelia remained mute and wide-eyed as her grandmother continued to elaborate on her strategy.

"I'll try to track down those living folks who might be responsible for dropping off any of the relics we have encountered in today's attic search. Then we will start picking a few brains for additional clues. As far as one Amelia Currick Gale is concerned, I am seriously considering asking your cousin Matt to help us out. The last I've heard, the University of Virginia is still located in Virginia, and not far from Richmond. Maybe he would be willing to search the vital records for the three names found in the chest. How does that sound to you?"

"Well, Granny Lou, Matt certainly has no problem keeping his grades up. Knowing him, he would have to be hard pressed to turn down a good mystery."

"So, we agree; I will contact him as soon as possible. Now, my dear Amelia, you are in charge of categorizing the information we have discovered thus far. That includes the old photos, family bibles, and whatever else is in this heap. I have cardboard file boxes which should work just fine for that purpose. Oh, and thank you so much for helping your old Granny Lou clean up her attic."

CHAPTER 9

The Search

att McDowell wasn't at all surprised to receive an early morning phone call from his Granny Lou. Ever since he could remember she had been an active player in the lives of all three of her grandchildren. Though, he had to admit that this phone call was not what he would have expected.

"Okay, Granny Lou, let me get this straight; you want me to access the names of three women who lived in Richmond during the nineteenth century?"

"Yes, Matt. Your mother mentioned that you planned to stay in Virginia over the winter school break. Of course, should you be too busy with your school work, I want you to say so. I certainly understand."

Matt was intrigued. Though he had planned to assist one of his professors with a research project, he felt he would have some time for the unexpected request. Besides, he would do just about anything for his Granny Lou and his cousin, Amelia. "Granny Lou, can you tell me more about the mystery, before I commit to you my powers of investigation. You know, this is a far cry from molecular science and the work I have been steeped in over the past three years.

Lou spewed out the limited information she and Amelia had discovered concerning the three women in question. "Matt, you were always a quick study from the time I sat you on my knee and taught you to read. Now, you shouldn't have a problem with this. I would start with the vital records, including the census records. Should that be a dead end, you might try sifting through the local genealogical and historical society libraries. I am uncertain which records would have survived the four years of Civil War."

"Okay, Granny Lou, anything for you and Amelia. By the way, how are she and Aunt Karen doing? Is Amelia back to playing the piano?"

"No, we are not there yet, small steps first. She has already begun to follow-up on the other woman who shares her name. I believe she is genuinely excited that Amelia Currick Gale might be the earliest ancestor to date that she has a common bond with. As for Karen, she continues to stay ahead of her demons. I believe this is all encouraging!"

Matt felt a sense of guarded relief. "I'm so glad that Amelia is responding positively to your improvisational therapy."

Before ending their conversation, Matt felt obliged to update his Granny Lou on his latest academic accomplishments. Though only twenty years of age, the sensitive lad was not lost to the love and pride his grandmother held for him.

*   *   *   *

Two weeks following Matt's telephone conversation with his grandmother, he had successfully completed the first semester of his junior year. As fate would have it, he was grateful for the diversionary research his grandmother had requested of him. Friends who had planned to remain on campus over winter break had decided to return to their homes, instead. This left Matt with more than adequate time to work on the biochemical research he was committed to, as well as help his Granny Lou.

The plan was to begin Granny Lou's project as soon as possible. Matt realized he did not have a clue as to where Richmond's vital records were housed. Rather quickly he pulled up the necessary information on his computer. Mumbling to himself he forged ahead. "Okay, now how do I get to the Richmond Health Department, from Charlottesville? Here we go, road directions leading me right to the front door, yes!"

Matt estimated that the drive to the Richmond Health Department from the dorm would take him an hour and a half. Considering his inexperience in this area, he concluded he would save himself time and aggravation by driving to Richmond rather than attempting to retrieve information via the internet or a letter. Fortunately, Lou had the foresight to advance Matt monies for the purpose of document retrieval and travel expenses.

The next day Matt was on the road headed northeast toward Richmond. During the drive his thoughts drifted back to his childhood. He clearly remembered the day when his dad and Uncle Ken had taken him, his brother and Amelia, to the local New Haven ice skating rink. The rink was always crowded during the Christmas holidays, and on this day the building resonated with the sound of steel scraping through ice.

He had to smile, when he recalled the tagalong party, slipping and sliding, as they tried to keep up with Uncle Ken. It seemed as though there was nothing Uncle Ken could not do.

In the solitude of his 1992 Chevy, the smile left Matt's smooth face, and tears rolled down his cheeks. He could not stop thinking how unfair life could be. It gnawed at him that his Uncle Ken had been dealt such a bad hand.

Matt's thoughts fueled his determination to follow through with Granny Lou's dubious plan to rescue Amelia. He had learned years earlier not to question his grandmother's judgment when it came to family matters. If his grandmother believed this effort would help Amelia to heal, this would probably be the case, or so he hoped! Matt eased his foot off the accelerator as he turned onto the exit leading to Richmond.

He drove as far as 1601 Willow Lawn Drive, where he came to a stop in front of the non-imposing, Virginia Department of Health. With his expectations soaring, he climbed the few steps leading to the main atrium. After checking the building directory he found his way to Suite 275. Within the large receiving room, he joined a short line of people standing in wait of the triage clerk. While he patiently waited, Matt tried to imagine the amount of information stored within the walls of this solitary building. He found irony in the thought, that the major events in the lives of so many people had been laid to rest and lost within these very walls.

Following a short wait Matt found himself standing before a middle aged, brown skinned woman. Pointedly, she questioned him as to the purpose of his visit.

Nervously, Matt fumbled to show the clerk his Connecticut driver's license. "The posted instructions said that you required some form of identification in order to access a vital record. I am interested in obtaining birth certificates for three individuals who were born sometime in the early 1800's."

The clerk ever so slightly lowered her eyes before replying. "I'm afraid that birth and death records housed within this building include those between 1853-1896, as well as those for June 1912 to present. I'm sorry we cannot help you, Sir."

Matt blushed, feeling as though his super sleuth persona had somehow been tarnished. How could he have ignored one of the elementary rules governing research of any nature. Namely, learn what information is available, where to find it, and how it can be best accessed. When he spoke, he continued to chastise himself. "That's what I get for impulsively setting off on a wild goose chase. Probably there is a wealth of information available on my computer in the peace and quiet of my dorm room!"

Matt's embarrassment and disappointment was transparent, and the clerk responded sympathetically. "Look, all is not lost, why don't you take a trip over to the Virginia Archives, located within the Library of Virginia. They may be able to help you continue with your search." Efficiently, she jotted down the address and wished him well.

Matt brightened up. "Thank you for your help." On his way out the door, he entertained the possibility that looking for dead relations might not be as easy as eyeing chemical reactions under the microscope. Methodically, he decided that if all else failed, he would fall back upon Granny Lou's advice, and begin searching the secondary sources. Though, for the moment he would once again try to access the primary sources in order to determine if the three women had begun their lives in the Richmond area.

With a new respect for the Sunday genealogist, Matt maneuvered his car through the congested Richmond streets. Eventually, he found his way to 8th Street, where he entered the library parking deck. After collecting his parking ticket from the dispenser he made his way to the Main lobby of the library. Still struggling with feelings of inadequacy, he awkwardly explained the reason for his visit to the library receptionist.

As directed, he proceeded to the Reference Library. Once again, he marveled at the volume of information, he was certain, must be housed within this 54,000 square foot, three-story building. Matt picked up his pace. Upon reaching his destination, he kept his eyes peeled for a Mrs. Singer, who he was told would assist him with his research. As he approached a large mahogany desk dominating the center of the room, he discreetly glanced at the name tag of the woman now seated three feet in front of him. Before she spoke he knew he had found Alice Singer.

The woman's dark, knowing eyes, gazed up at the lanky, young sleuth. "Can I help you, young man?" She continued before Matt could answer. "If you are looking for a lost ancestor, I need to see a picture ID. You will also be required to complete this registration form before you may access our materials. If all is satisfactory, and you are able to provide me with the: Who, What, Where, When and Why of your search, I will take it from there. If you have limited information, just give me what you do know."

Matt handed Mrs. Singer both his Connecticut driver's license as well as his picture ID from the University of Virginia. When he completed the registration form, Mrs. Singer, with practiced efficiency, gathered up the form and Matt's student ID. "I will not need your driver's license, your student ID will suffice." She proceeded to xerox a copy of Matt's ID, while repeating her request for specific information.

The limited information available to Matt, spilled from his lips. "The names are Amelia Currick Gale, Adelaide Gale, and Mazzie Winfield. The women lived sometime between 1830 and the Civil War years. I have cause to believe that they lived within the Richmond area or in its close proximity."

"We certainly have volumes of information for the Richmond area. Since you do not know the exact birth dates of the women you are looking for, and because they are all female, I would suggest that you search the census record first. Prior to 1853, Virginia did not collect any other vital statistics. A good place to start would be the 1850 Census Records. This is available on microfilm." Without taking a breath, Mrs. Singer continued. "By beginning with the 1850 census, you will find a list of the names of all individuals in the household on the day the census was taken. Age, sex, race, and other types of information will appear as well. Prior to 1850, only the name of the head of the household is provided for. This information is then followed by a numerical count of other categories of individuals living under the same roof. For example, categories might include free white males and females, slaves and free blacks."

Though Matt's initial plan had been to begin his search ten

or twenty years earlier, Mrs. Singer's suggestion made sense to him, so he nodded in agreement.

Expeditiously, she made arrangements to have the microfilm retrieved from the archives. "Matt, please let me know if you need my assistance once you have found applicable information. You might want me to help you take your search a step further. I noticed that you have your laptop with you; if you like, I will approve it for library use."

"Oh, yes, that would be great, thank you!" Matt thought that Mrs. Singer seemed to think of everything.

Pointing with her finger, Mrs. Singer gave Matt his last instruction. "Okay, now just take a seat in the far end of the room and I will bring you the microfilm."

Matt seated himself at one of the tables, which had the necessary equipment for viewing microfilm. He felt a sense of relief, believing he might actually be on the verge of uncovering the first clue to the family mystery.

Within minutes, Mrs. Singer returned with three spools of microfilm. "I imagine that you are familiar with using the viewer?"

With a knowing smile, Matt assured the librarian of his proficiency. "My studies at UVA have more than prepared me."

Mrs. Singer nodded and smiled in return. "Well, yes, I should have known better then to have even asked. You see, my daughter also attends UVA. I will leave you now, to your own devices."

After placing the microfilm in the viewer, Matt found the census to be amazingly thorough, just as Mrs. Singer had suggested. Mumbling to himself Matt's eyes scrolled down the listed demographics. "Let's see, we have the names of household members, their age, sex, race, occupation, value of their estate, birthplace, marriage within year, school within year, literary status, and enumeration date. Who, could ask for more!"

Methodically, Matt skipped to the surnames beginning

with the letter G. He immediately eyed the Gale family name. There were but three Gale families listed, so perusal was fast and effortless. He focused his attention on the name Malin Gale, finding that family members matched the names of two of the women whose lives he was attempting to uncover.

At the time of the census, the family patriarch had been forty-one years of age. Family members included his thirty-five year old wife, Adelaide, two sons, Justin, sixteen years of age, and ten years old, Everton. Youngest of the children, was six year old, Amelia Currick Gale. "Yes!" Matt whispered under his breath. "Could anything get better than this?"

Eagerly, Matt read on. Malin Gale's occupation was cited as planter, owning a considerable fortune in tobacco real estate. According to the census, during colonial times his fortune had been valued at 1,500,000 dollars. Matt thought it strange that while Justin and Everton's birthplace had been recorded as Richmond, Virginia, records indicated that Amelia had been born in Roanoke, Virginia. As he expected, all members of the family could read and write.

Lost to his thoughts, Matt wondered where his search would take him next. His last conscious recollection of time occurred at 2:00 PM, when he had stepped into the library lobby. As he paused to look at his watch he caught the sight of Mrs. Singer heading in his direction. Though smiling, she remained the epitome of professionalism. "Well, young man, have you had much success with your search?"

Matt could barely contain his excitement. "Most definitely, though I still have some digging to do."

Looking, not in the least bit surprised, Mrs. Singer spoke. "That is wonderful, but I'm sorry to remind you that we close the reference rooms at 4:30 PM. It sounds like you might be returning tomorrow?"

Matt looked surprised over the amount of time which had escaped his notice. "Oh, yes, of course. I mean, ah, yes, the time; and I will indeed be returning tomorrow. Here is your microfilm, and thank you so much for all your help."

Matt sensed the same euphoria he had experienced, when accepted at UVA. With a bounce in his step, he made his way to the parking garage. He wondered where he might rent a room for the night. It seemed impractical to drive back to his dorm only to return the following morning. He decided that the best course of action would be to question the parking attendant.

The elderly attendant flashed a broad smile as he collected Matt's parking fee. Then in a gravelly, though cordial voice, he directed Matt to one of the nearest motels.

All but a few blocks from the library, Matt found the Comfort Inn Midtown. He checked in and hurried to his room. More than ready to share the day's success with Granny Lou, he immediately dialed up her number. Following four rings, he heard his grandmother's teasing voice. "What kept you so long?"

Nearly breathless, Matt told his Granny Lou, what he had discovered concerning the Gale family history.

Lou sounded jubilant. "Nice work, Matt!"

"Wait there is more. The family resided in Charles City, a stretch of land near the James River. The area is situated between Richmond and Williamsburg. You know this is actually fun! Tomorrow, I will return to the library and begin accessing the secondary sources. I can't wait to get my hands on some of the old newspapers; I bet there are volumes on this prominent family. Possibly, I will learn something about Mazzie Winfield, as well."

Lou's voice reflected Matt's excitement. "Wait until I tell Amelia about your success. Keep digging deeper, Matt. If possible, try to find the names of living relatives in the area. They may have additional knowledge about the family history. I know I am jumping ahead of myself, but I have a good feeling about this. It looks as though Amelia and I may be heading South in the very near future."

Chapter 10

Assistant Extraordinaire

E arly the following morning, Matt returned to the library. For the first time he took note of the looming burnt sienna walls. The color only fueled his vision of a well fed bookworm on the verge of devouring yet another gourmet meal. Not that he would openly admit to any similarities. The preposterous thought only served to propel him faster toward the reference room. With determination, if not a plan, he approached the reference desk. His eyes immediately sought out the stern, though reassuring face of Mrs. Singer. To his surprise, he found the face of a much younger woman. She looked up at him with Mrs. Singer's same dark piercing eyes, though he thought the face much softer and prettier. "Hello," he said, "I am looking for Mrs. Singer."

"Oh, you must be Matt McDowell, my mother mentioned that you were planning to come by today to continue with your genealogical research. She is at a meeting this morning; I 'm her daughter, Lisa Singer. When not attending classes, I often help out at the library. My mother specifically asked me to offer you my assistance. I am recognized as the genealogy sleuth of Richmond."

"Pleased, to meet you, Lisa. I am flattered that your mother remembered that I would be returning."

"Oh, she does not forget much. Besides she is always on the lookout for brainy, good looking, young men who might be the perfect catch for her unattached daughter."

Matt's freckles appeared to converge as his skin flushed a crimson red. A testament to the fact, that Matt's experience with the ladies, was as limited as his knowledge of genealogy.

Lisa mischievously smiled. "You know, this has gotten out of hand. Matt, I'm sure my mother's intent was for me to offer you my help, if you so desire. Just forget about the other nonsense."

"Well, Lisa if you are as good at genealogy research as you are at spreading the blarney, I believe I could use your help. Aren't you required to help other library patrons in need of your assistance?"

Flirtatiously, Lisa replied. "Be pre-warned, should a magnificently endowed young man with a string of degrees after his name, present himself as needing the assistance of a seasoned archivist, I shall spit you out like a hot jalapeno pepper. Just more blarney, I assure you. Mrs. Carney, is actually the assistant reference librarian, who will render help to other curious seekers. Despite my considerable talent, I usually end up returning books and microfilm to their waiting niches. Besides, I was told that we attend the same school. With that in your favor, I would be pleased to help you continue with your research."

Collecting his wits, Matt nonchalantly gave Lisa the okay. Following his assistant's strange introduction, he was more than ready to get started. "I'm trying to locate secondary source information on a prominent nineteenth century family who lived in Charles City. The surname is Gale, more specifically the Malin Gale family. Where would be a good place to begin?"

Lisa twirled a strand of her short wavy hair around her index finger. "Well, I would imagine that if Mr. Gale was a prominent citizen of Charles City, he probably owned land in the area, and possibly elsewhere, as well."

"Oh yes, according to the census, Malin's real estate was worth a whopping $1,500,000.00. The census indicated that his land produced most of the tobacco crop for the state of Virginia."

"Well, things have not changed that much; with land ownership there will always be taxes." Lisa knowingly smiled. "Let's explore the tax records and expand on the information you already have. Tax records will often give you an idea of where the land holdings are located, as well as who might have inherited the estate following a death. In all likelihood, the land holdings will be in the hands of his descendents. Write out your slip request for the 1850 through 1900 tax records; we will see what we come up with."

Matt was grateful for Lisa's prompt return. "That was quick, let's see what we have." Together, they placed the microfilm into the viewer and with little effort found the 1850 tax record for Malin Gale. It was noted that his name appeared on the tax records from 1850 through 1869. Property ownership included Galynn Hall, a manor house situated on the James River. The estate encompassed 684 acres of land, located within Charles City, an outgrowth of Richmond.

Lisa's voice became animated. "My, oh my, look at this. Mr. Gale was certainly well heeled. In addition to the Charles City property he owned 1,850 acres of land within Roanoke County. Apparently, there had been a home and other buildings on the Roanoke property."

"Well, if the guy was a tobacco farmer he would have to own a good deal of land. That also explains why Amelia Currick Gale's birthplace is recorded as Roanoke County." Matt's face showed his obvious satisfaction.

Lisa, not to be upstaged by her protégé, added. "Now,

this is interesting, in 1870 ownership of all land holdings appear as the Malin Gale estate. Apparently Mr. Gale had died somewhere between 1869 and 1870. The 1871 tax list show both the Charles City and the Roanoke County properties as being in the hands of his eldest son, Justin. That's funny, since in 1779, Thomas Jefferson rewrote the state legal code in order to abolish primogeniture and entail, as forms of land inheritance."

"Lisa, please put that into English for an ignorant science major."

"Oh, I'm sorry, Matt! All that means is that land inheritance could no longer be automatically passed down to the eldest son."

Matt looked puzzled. "Why then, would Adelaide and the other children be left out of the inheritance? Unless, they had not survived the devastation during the Civil War. Well, anyway, before I can establish Amelia Currick Gale as a Thomas family ancestor, we will have to uncover what had happened to her during and after the war."

Lisa looked puzzled. "What do you mean a Thomas family ancestor?"

Matt frowned. "Oh, nothing, I will explain this to you later."

"Well, whatever, let's just continue with the tax lists and see where that takes us."

"Look Lisa, apparently the Roanoke land had been sold off along with half of the acreage in Charles City. Only 342 acres just adjacent to Galynn Hall remain in family hands."

Lisa beamed. "Most definitely, ownership lies with Elizabeth Gale Bissett. She is the offspring of Winston and Edith Gale, direct descendents of Justin Gale.

Matt, impulsively stopped. "Listen Lisa, would you continue here on your own, while I focus upon obtaining a physical address for Galynn Hall and the Bissett family?"

"Not, at all. You might try the popular web site which lists

Richmond's historic plantations. Go across the room and plug your computer in for internet access and you should be good to go!" Lisa smiled.

"Thanks, I'll be right back." Matt, with laptop in hand, quickly moved himself to the nearest hookup.

Within twenty minutes, Matt returned triumphantly. "Well, this should send Granny Lou into a state of ecstasy. I'll explain who Granny Lou is later. The Galynn Hall estate is located at 2847 John Tyler Highway. I imagine that is not very far from where we sit. Lisa, what time is it?"

Lisa looked at her watch. "It's already 11:45 AM. Time certainly flies by when you are consorting with the dead."

"How about we move on to the living and get a bite to eat? Lunch is on me, of course." Matt surprised himself, was he really willing to break away from the research?

Lisa's face reflected Matt's surprise. "Well, don't you want to continue; this is just the beginning? We still have to find out what happened to Justin's siblings. That means we need to take a look at military records, news clippings and other secondary information."

Matt persevered. "Of course, the research is not over. If you are available to help me this afternoon, we will start looking up those sources for more information. In the mean time, I would like to learn more about my pretty, as well as tenacious assistant. So are you free for lunch?"

Lisa's response was spontaneous. "Now, who's spewing the blarney? Even so, it is agreeable blarney. I am free for lunch and afternoon research, on one condition."

Matt looked cautious. "Okay, what is your condition?"

"Well, I need to know more about you, as well. Starting with why you are researching the Gale family? Why aren't you home getting ready for the Christmas holiday?" Lisa sounded resolute.

"Is that all? Well, of course, Lisa. You deserve to know what this is all about. Now, can we go?"

"Yes, let me just write a short note to my mom; I don't think she is back from her meeting. Believe it or not, she still worries when she does not know where I am and who I am with. I have refrained from rebelling, and have found it easier to comply with her wishes." Lisa spoke a few words to Mrs. Carney and handed her the note.

Together, the young couple made their way out to the street. Greeted by an aerosol of cold December air, they quickened their step, which only heightened their exuberance. Lisa lead the way to the Eagle's Nest, an eatery not far from the looming State Capitol Building.

The mood was upbeat and even the cool green leather booth seemed cozy and inviting to the couple. Over an order of hamburgers and fries, Lisa's curiosity resurfaced. "So Matt, why are you researching the Gale family? I know by now that the research is more than a simple class project."

Matt hesitated. "Oh, no you don't; before I give away family secrets I need to know something about my research assistant. So, let's start with you! What are you majoring in at UVA, and how did you come to be such a practiced genealogist?"

"Well, okay," Lisa began coyly. "My name is Lisa Singer and I am currently in my sophomore year at UVA, majoring in Art History. As you already know, my mother Alice, is the head librarian at the Library of Virginia. She has taught me all she knows in the area of genealogical research; which is quite a bit, I might add. Actually, my sideline, ties in nicely with Art History. You learn so much about dead people through their artifacts and works of art, don't you think? Well, anyway, my wonderful dad has his full professorship and teachers at the University of Richmond. I aspire to follow in his footsteps some day and teach at UVA." Lisa flashed that same mischievous smile, Matt had seen earlier in the day. "For the most part, I am your typical Jewish Southern belle, weighing in at 120 pounds, measuring 67 inches tall, with expressive large brown eyes and short dark hair. Oh, yes, I have never been featured on America's most wanted. Now, you please."

Matt stroked his chin, more like a Dutch uncle than a young college student. "You are a hard act to follow; let me see. As you already know, I am in my junior year at UVA, majoring in molecular biology. I plan to work in the field of biochemical research. My family stems from New Haven, Connecticut. Like yourself, I am blessed with a wonderful mom and dad, as well as a younger brother. Andrew, by the way, is the lucky chap who has inherited the family good looks. Also to his credit, is an aptitude for sports, as well as the fact he is a charismatic fellow. On the other hand, I am tied to the books both on and off campus. Physically, I would describe myself as lean, though in no way mean. At my last weigh in, I topped the scale at 165 pounds of flesh covering a 5'10" frame. As you can see I have perfectly straight teeth, thick strawberry blond hair, and my mother tells me I have beautiful blue eyes."

Lisa quickly interjected. "Well, I agree with your mother. So once again, tell me why are you spending your winter vacation delving into the old bones of the Gale family?"

"Now, this is where my life gets interesting!" Matt slowly and deliberately told Lisa all he felt she needed to know about his cousin Amelia and the loss of her father in the 9/11 World Trade Center attack. He talked about his Granny Lou and how she believed that Amelia would benefit through momentarily losing herself to a search for those ancestors for whom she had been named.

Lisa remained uncommonly quiet, listening intently. Matt was not lost to the tears welling up within the young woman's soulful brown eyes. "Oh, Matt, that must be so terrible for Amelia and your family. Please know I will continue to make myself available to you in researching the Gale family. Now, what do you say we get back to work?"

*　　*　　*　　*

Alice Singer greeted Lisa and Matt upon their return to the Reference Library. "Well, I see you two have been getting acquainted. How is the research going?"

With mutual zeal, the couple responded simultaneously. Good, really, good!"

Lisa took the lead in reviewing for her mother what the couple had discovered. Mrs. Singer looked pleased. "You have made significant headway. I would suggest you try to track down Everton Gale next. In all likelihood, he and his brother Justin had served in the Confederate Army. If luck stays with you, finding the fate of Everton might involve little if any work at all. Well, you had better get started."

In response to Mrs. Singer's praise Lisa and Matt beamed like two third graders. "Okay, you heard your mother, let's get started. Where do we go from here, Lisa?"

Lisa required little coaxing. "I say we head over to the computer room and access the library database for the Virginia Military Dead. This is a particularly good database as it pulls together information from several other sources. This will spare us the time and energy it takes to access the other sources individually."

Through the recommended database, Matt went on to access the American Civil War Dead. "Oh good, the names are alphabetically listed, this should go fairly quick. Lisa, look at this! Only two with the Gale surname; and one just happens to be an Everton Gale!"

Lisa pushed in closer to the computer screen. "You are right! It seems our Everton was a Confederate 1st Lieutenant in General Lee's Army of Northern Virginia."

Matt felt a rush of excitement. "Lisa, please continue reading!"

"Apparently, he had been wounded in action while defending Richmond, in the offensive at Cold Harbor, against Grant's Army of the Potomac. He suffered a fatal head wound on June 1, 1864, and was laid to rest in the family cemetery. Matt, that's about it."

"Lisa, I could kiss you! Not only did we learn lickety-split about Everton's fate, we now know that the family had its own cemetery. Cemeteries don't always bury its family secrets. Now, let's get started on unraveling the fate of Amelia Currick Gale."

"Matt, aren't you going to first write down the findings and the name of the source?" Pragmatically, Lisa continued. "Let's get a copy of the Military Dead Record, containing the information about Everton. Then record on your writing tab, the source, date of the find, and place we located the info."

With uncharacteristic levity, Matt attempted to make light of his oversight. "But of course, I am just playing dumb so you will feel needed and not desert me in the middle of this."

Lisa rolled her big eyes. "Don't worry, I shan't do that. Now, let's go over the Death Records once again, before looking in the secondary sources for Ms. Amelia. There is always the chance she did not live through the Civil War. The state of Virginia began recording deaths, as well as marriages, as early as 1853. Prior to 1853, we will have to rely on local church records and other secondary sources. I'll be right back."

Before Matt could respond, Lisa was off to retrieve the necessary microfilm.

The rest of the day was spent in a thorough review of both the death and marriage records for the Richmond area. The name Amelia Currick Gale was not to be found within either of the records.

"Well, Lisa, it is 3:30 PM and nothing so far. Maybe, now would be a good time to start delving into the secondary sources."

With a grimace, Lisa agreed. "Yes, I think you are right. Though, I have to leave now; I have a family commitment in the early evening. But, I will return the following morning to give you a hand, if you plan to continue the research."

Matt's chin dropped in disappointment. "Oh, okay, I'll just continue solo for the next hour and a half."

Though Lisa continued to reassure Matt, he sensed her devilish enjoyment at the sight of his forlorn demeanor. "Don't worry your assistant will meet you at 9:00 AM sharp in the Reference Library. Here is my home phone number if for any reason your plans change." Lisa's lips curved into a pretty smile. "Thanks for lunch, and your stimulating company."

Matt blushed and smiled back as Lisa left the room. The search through several years of death and marriage records had left Matt feeling fatigued on many levels. Believing, that tackling the secondary sources would be less taxing, he decided to spend the rest of the day in that direction.

Within minutes of Lisa's departure, he moved himself into the area of the library which housed periodicals and newspapers, dating back as early as the 1800s. Matt was glad that this area of the building remained open to the public a half an hour later than the adjoining Reference Library. Wasting little time, he quickly accessed the catalog of local newspapers. Scanning the list of newspapers available to Richmond citizenry during the 1850s and 1860s, he identified the *Richmond Dispatch* as a likely source of period news. The *Richmond Dispatch* made claim to some 1,800 readers during this time in history. It had been the most widely read and circulated newspaper in the area. The paper had been printed Monday through Saturday, with a traditional four-page format until the summer of 1862. After which, it had shortened its edition to two pages, with the exception of its Saturday paper, which remained a four-page edition. Easy and fast perusal of the paper was made possible due to its brevity. Matt began reading the microfilm which stored copies of the 1850 newsprint. As he read he soon learned that six years old, Amelia continued in good health, living with her family during this time.

In large part due to the Gale family's wealth and prominence, the family had been cited in several of the newspaper editions. During the years between 1850 and 1859, Matt had found several articles of interest. Most of these articles were located within the context of page one under *'Local Matters'*. These articles pertained to the production of tobacco in the area, elaborating upon problems stemming from weather conditions and the shortage of slave labor. Malin Gale had been cited as the foremost grower of tobacco in the region and a vocal proponent for improved ways in which to harvest the labor-intensive crop. As pointed out by Mr. Gale, the crop remained the mainstay of Virginia's economy, and its continued production was imperative to the State's economic well-being.

Finally, within the September 1860 edition, Matt found an article pertaining solely to Amelia Currick Gale. The feature article discussed the annual social cotillion to be held that same month in Williamsburg. The annual event had been held alternately, in Williamsburg, Washington DC, or Richmond. As explained, the cotillion provided the opportunity for prominent families to introduce their daughters to prospective husbands of the same ilk. At the age of sixteen, Amelia Currick Gale was to be presented at the cotillion, as were three other young ladies from the area. Matt stared at the still distinguishable photo of the young women. He was quick to note that Amelia Currick Gale, not unlike his young cousin, had had more than her share of physical charms.

Matt continued to read. When he reached the title page of the last edition, his eyes nearly left their sockets. Mirrored up to him from the December 1, 1860 edition were the words, *Daughter of Malin Gale, Missing.* Matt remained glued to the viewfinder. The article continued, explaining events leading up to the young woman's strange disappearance from Galynn Hall. It had stated that Mistress Gale's maid servant, Mazzie Winfield had disappeared as well, and was believed to be somehow culpable.

On page three of the same edition, amidst advertisements

describing the individual characteristics of several runaway slaves, was the name Mazzie Winfield. Mazzie was described as a handsome light mulatto woman of twenty-one years of age, who pronounced her words easily. It was mentioned that she was a skilled seamstress. The third sentence strongly alluded to her likely involvement with the disappearance. A reward of $ 500.00 had been offered for the apprehension and delivery of the house slave. An additional $ 500.00 would be awarded for any reliable information concerning the disappearance of Miss Amelia.

Matt muttered to himself. "So that explains why Mazzie's name had not appeared in the census, nor anywhere else, for that matter." He knew now that she had been a slave, and in the eyes of the law, considered nothing more than someone's property.

Remembering, Lisa's suggestion, Matt made note of all news editions which had made reference to the Gale family. Then, he packed up his belongings and headed for his motel room, eager to report back to Granny Lou.

CHAPTER 11

Family Ties

How Lou hated when her mind refused to move from the hold of a promise, whether her own or someone else's. Throughout the evening meal she had refrained from her usual chatter, and Mike was left to deal with her pensiveness. As she stacked the meal's dirty dishes, to her enormous relief, the phone rang. "Oh, that is probably Matt." Flustered, she searched high and low for a hand towel. "Now, where is that doggone towel?"

"Calm down, I'll get it while you dry off." Mike casually picked up the kitchen phone. Lou rolled her eyes, well aware that her husband would never admit to his own curiosity concerning the Amelia Currick Gale saga.

"Hi there, Matt, how are things going for you? So what tantalizing news do you have for us, today? Your grandmother is darn near ready to jump out of her skin in anticipation of your call." Before Matt could answer his grandfather, Lou picked up the phone in the study and began her own barrage of questions.

In an uncommonly big voice, Matt interrupted his

grandparents. "Okay, slow down you two and give me a chance to fill you in on all we have discovered."

For Lou, Matt's words held a dichotomy of interest. "What do you mean we, who are we?"

Matt would not be distracted. "Oh, not now, Granny Lou; I will get back to that matter in due time. Do you have something to write with?" Triumphantly, the Bissett name and the Galynn Hall address spilled from Matt's lips. It sounded as though Matt had stopped breathing during his twenty minute critique of what he and Lisa had uncovered concerning Amelia Currick Gale and her family.

"The good news is we know that the young woman in question had reached her sixteenth birthday. Just prior to the outbreak of the Civil War, she disappeared from the lap of southern comfort. Unfortunately, there are no apparent clues as to why she left, or where she had gone."

Brimming over with excitement, Lou interjected. "So what next, Matt; are you finished there?"

"No, I am planning on spending one more day in Richmond. Oh, the 'we', you questioned me about, is none other than Ms. Lisa Singer, research assistant extraordinaire. Together, we plan to peruse the 19th century newspapers in the hope of uncovering any other newsworthy information pertaining to the Gale family. Then, I'll head back to campus tomorrow evening."

With considerable restraint, Lou refrained from questioning Matt further about Lisa Singer. She knew that should Matt want to share specifics about his assistant, he would do so in his own time.

"Oh, Matt, before you hang up, you should know that Amelia and I have established an irrefutable lineage between Amelia Currick Gale and the Thomas family. We know for a fact that she ended up in our neck of the woods, marrying my Great-Great-Grandfather Edan Thomas and bearing him two healthy sons.

Matt sounded surprised. "It would seem that you and

Amelia are one step ahead of me; will you still be traveling to Richmond in the near future?"

"Yes, Matt, as soon as the holidays are over I will begin coordinating our trip. Hopefully, Mrs. Bissett will agree to meet with us. It is more than likely she has information that will shed light upon circumstances behind our great-great-grandmother's mysterious curtain call from her southern home." Lou continued. "Matt, within two short days, you and your assistant have done a wonderful job. Please let me know if you come up with anything else you believe is important, possibly the names of other distant relatives living in the area. Be careful in your travels, I love you."

Mike had continued to listen on the kitchen extension throughout the conversation. Only now, was he able to slide in a few parting words. "That goes for me too, Matt, I love you guy. Goodbye."

Lou beamed with pride, as she stepped back into the kitchen. "What an amazing boy; I can't wait to tell Amelia about these latest developments."

Mike cautioned his wife. "Honey, don't you think that at this time of the evening, Amelia might be involved with school assignments? Didn't Karen agree to allow Amelia the opportunity to participate in the genealogy project only if it did not prove a distraction from her school work? Maybe, it would be best to wait and call tomorrow."

Lou grimaced, she knew Mike was right, and secretly resented his common sense. She remembered how with typical tenacity she had convinced Karen that a change of focus might very well serve as a side door out of Amelia's perceived problems. The final decision, as to whether Amelia would be permitted to work on the project, rested upon the teenager's past success in juggling school work with piano practice. Of course, Amelia had not voiced any objection to her involvement.

It did not take long before Lou decided that her need to speak with Amelia, out weighted Mike's common sense.

Sheepishly, she began to dial up her daughter's telephone number. Preferring not to explain herself to Karen, she crossed her fingers and mumbled under her breath. "Come on Amelia, answer the phone!"

*   *   *   *

Normally, Amelia was no slouch when it came to talking on the telephone, this evening she found its piercing ring downright annoying. Animal, plant, or mineral, she did not feel much like talking. Once again, she had fallen from her mother's good graces. Realizing that her refusal to answer the phone would only make matters worse, she picked up the demonic instrument. "Hello, oh, Granny Lou, I'm so glad it is you! I'm not in the mood for much conversation right now."

"Oh dear, I'm sorry I caught you at a bad time. Ah, can I help with anything?"

Only after her grandmother stumbled through her second sentence did Amelia regret her curtness. "Granny Lou, would you love me if I were ugly, and had only four digits on either hand, making it impossible for me to play the piano?"

"But of course! Besides you would never be ugly to those that love you, and your talent for the piano is but a gift from God. Only you can decide whether you want to cultivate that gift."

Amelia appreciated her grandmother's wisdom. "Why are grandmothers so much smarter than mothers?"

"Dear, they are not necessarily smarter, maybe older and more practiced. Now, what is going on between you and your mother?"

Amelia did not try to hide her exasperation, breathing a long tortured sigh into the phone. "The same old, same old!"

"I guess your mother has once again requested that you practice your piano? Amelia, tell me why don't you enjoy playing your music anymore?"

Amelia hesitated. "Granny Lou, I don't really know for

sure. It once made me so happy, and now a great sadness come over me when I play. I don't even want to talk about it."

"Well, we don't have to talk about it right now. Although, now I don't know if this is a good time to share my wonderful news with you."

"Granny Lou, wonderful news would be very refreshing. What is it?"

Without wasting any time, Lou raced on with what Matt had reported. "I would like for us both to visit with Elizabeth Gale Bissett at her home in Charles City. Of course, I will need time to contact the woman. I hope she will agree to meet with us. Well, what do you say?"

Amelia jumped at the opportunity. "Anything, to get out of this house! Besides, in comparison with my other namesakes, Amelia Currick Gale remains a real mystery. Don't you think?"

"Yes, I certainly do! This is why I am so excited." Lou immediately returned to her proposed plan. "So what do you think; could you get away from your school work?"

"Well, I am sure a trip to Richmond over the Christmas vacation is out. Mom has my vacation time packed full of activities; but, of course, I want to go with you."

Lou interjected. "The winter holidays would not work anyway. It is doubtful I could set up a meeting that quickly. I am certain Mrs. Bissett's calendar is as full as our own. First, let me go about trying to get in touch with her. Maybe after I get some tentative dates, your mother will agree to let you take off a few days from school. We will be traveling only about 400 miles to Richmond."

Amelia maintained her usual cool. Though, she had to admit, if only to herself, that the family mystery was becoming most intriguing. Nonchalantly, she replied. "That would be fine with me. Well, I have to go; I love you Granny Lou! Oh, I guess we will see you on Monday for our shopping trip?"

"Oh, my goodness, I almost forgot about the shopping

trip! I can't believe it is all but seven days until Christmas. I had better talk with your mother; where is she anyway? Oh, before you hang up, I hope you realized how very much your mother loves you!"

"Yes Granny Lou, I know. Maybe that is why she is so hard to live with. I'll see if mom is finished with her bath. Bye!"

*   *   *   *

Within seconds, Karen picked up the phone. "Hi Mom, has Amelia been giving you an ear full about how I continue to badger her about playing the piano?"

"Well, that certainly entered the conversation. Though, I did get a chance to discuss with her the reason for my call."

Karen only heard her mother's first sentence. Feeling on the defensive, she demanded her mother's equal time. "Mom, I just do not know what has happened to us since Ken's death. Amelia and I use to be so open and honest with one another; now, no matter what I say, or how I say it, I am suspect. This evening I casually mentioned that I would love for her to play some Mozart for me. No sooner had I finished my sentence, then the transformation from Angel Girl into sullen Bratzilla, ensued."

"Karen, please give it more time. There is so much going on here; give Amelia and yourself time to figure it out. You have both been through so much!"

Though Karen respected her mother's judgment, she believed that her mother's tolerance of Amelia's recalcitrance was somewhat indulgent. Her voice brimmed with resignation. "So, I guess I am the only one who thinks there is a problem!"

"No, that is not the case, dear! There may, or there may not be a problem. None of us knows but Amelia. I'm just asking you to give her the time to figure that out for herself. Then, trust that she will eventually share whatever she is experiencing, with you. I know this is difficult, I continue to work at it myself."

"Mom, I am just so exhausted. For everyone's sanity I promise I will try to be more patient with Amelia. Now, I know this is anticlimactic, but tell me why did you call?"

"Ah, well. I need to know what time you were planning to pick me up for our Christmas shopping excursion, this coming Monday."

Karen noted the hesitation in her mother's voice. "Ten in the morning would work. Mom, are you sure that is the only reason you called tonight?"

It took little coaxing, before Lou once again reiterated her last conversation with Matt.

"Karen smiled to herself. "I share in your excitement over the prospects of having family ties in Virginia. So, I guess you would like Amelia to drive to Richmond with you?"

"Now, you are reading your mother's mind."

"Okay, yes, why not. Amelia continues to do well in school and possibly a hiatus from one another would do us both a world of good."

CHAPTER 12

Christmas Again

Amelia watched from the backseat of her mother's car as a whirlwind of color bounded toward them. As her grandmother entered the vehicle, Amelia felt a gush of cold December air brush across her face.

"It's a little brisk out there. How are you, my dear?" Before Karen could respond, Granny Lou turned her attention to the backseat. "Amelia, don't you look delicious in that red jacket. Trish, what a pleasant surprise; how nice you are joining us. Are you girls itching to buy out the Macy's Department store?"

Karen interjected. "No Mom, we have all made a pact to refrain from over spending and to just buy one nice gift for one another. The rest of our holiday spend money will be given to our chosen charity. You might say, in keeping with the real meaning of Christmas."

Trish added. "You can tell we all heard the same sermon this past Sunday, *'Remember the Reason for the Season',* or something like that."

"Well, you youngsters are shaming your Granny Lou;

I'm the one who should be setting an example for you! Still, sometimes we are all a little naughty."

"Well, Mother that is the plan. We are all starting out with good intentions, we will see how it goes."

Lou wrinkled her nose. "I guess from hence forth I had better toe the line. Though, I would very much like to indulge my girls, even if only today. You are included as well, Trish."

Trish giggled. "Thank you, Mrs. McDowell. I'm always up for indulgence."

Amelia knowingly smiled at her friend. "Yes Trish, we know all about it."

*   *   *   *

Karen circled the Mount Pleasant Shopping Mall several times before spotting a parking space within the crowded lot. "Maybe I should have left you off at the entrance, it looks like we will have a bit of a trek."

Simultaneously, everyone expressed their willingness to walk the distance and in no time they entered the main entrance to the mega mall. Following a few seconds of thawing, Amelia and Trish announced their intention to shop on their own. That was Granny Lou's cue to repeat the logistical plan. "Remember, we will meet up at The Pumpkin House at 1 PM, for lunch."

Before trotting off, Amelia and Trish assured Granny Lou they would be on time for lunch. Then in a blink of an eye, Amelia led the way to Kelsey's Fine Jewelry.

"Melie, do you have anything specific in mind?"

"Yup, I want to buy a charm for my mom's charm bracelet." Amelia pointed out a gold charm replicating a small stack of books. "It's for the charm bracelet my dad gave her four or five years ago. Do you think she will like it?"

"Sure, why not. I see your mom wearing that bracelet, often. By the way, what would you like for Christmas?"

"Trish, you don't have to get me anything!"

Trish's jaw dropped. "What? Are you sick or something? We have always bought one another a gift."

"Well, don't worry; I still plan to surprise you with something." Amelia did not miss Trish's forlorn expression. "Look, if you insist on getting me something, how about buying this precious metal cleaner, and giving me that."

"What on earth are you going to do with that? Amelia, you just keep getting weirder and weirder."

"Thanks a lot. I just thought that someday I could clean up this old tarnished cross that Uncle Stew gave me for my sixteenth birthday." Amelia pointed to the cross bulging from under her sweater.

Trish snickered. "But of course, that makes sense. Well, if that is what you want, I'll buy it, wrap it and put a big red bow on the bottle. By the way everyone missed you this past Saturday evening."

Amelia dropped her eyes. "Oh, I meant to ask. How did the Christmas Pageant go?"

"Well, considering you're in retirement, and Ms. Cynthia Ambrose filled in for you, not bad. I confess, I was wishing she would flub up." Trish's face was full of disdain.

"Trish, why are you so nasty toward Cynthia? What did she ever do to you?

"Actually, nothing. Besides, it is almost Christmas and I am trying to control my ugliness."

Amelia eyeballed Trish. "Kind of late for that, don't you think? But I guess if you tolerate my weirdness, I'll tolerate your ugliness. Is it a deal?"

Both girls laughed at themselves. As far as Amelia was concerned, she was ready to put the conversation behind her.

The girls moseyed from the jewelry store into the open area of the shopping mall, where they encountered a throng of parents with their small children. Some of the children clung to their parents in dire fear, while others waited impatiently for their turn to sit on the lap of a large jolly man with a long white beard. At times the noise was deafening, though Amelia and Trish remained captivated by the sight.

"Melie, can you remember that far back, when you and I were one of those squirming, squealing kids waiting to tell Santa what we wanted for Christmas. It's hard to believe we actually believed in all that stuff, don't you think?"

"Oh, how I wish I could still believe in all that stuff. I remember being two or three, when my dad reassured me that Santa loved little children and was someone I could trust. With his reassurance, I marched right up to Santa and nestled in the girth of his large belly. Dad always took such good care of me and my mom; I miss him so much."

"Ya, your dad was a good guy; just like my dad. But, I still don't believe in the Santa Claus thing!"

Amelia looked at her friend incredulously. "Well, Trish, I would expect not. I said I wish I could still believe; but for Pete sake, we are practically adults. We would have to be simple minded to fall for that stuff."

Trish rolled her eyes. "That's for sure, after everything that's happened. Come on let's get going and finish our shopping before lunch."

Amelia was ready to move on, as well. "Okay, where to next?"

Trish did not hesitate. "Alright girl, get your money out, no surprises this year. We are going to Victoria's Secret. I saw this amazing push up bra in a magazine that I must have. A French lace bra, only one's very best friend would buy for her."

Amelia expressed her surprise. "It sounds like something a husband should buy; but, neither one of us has a husband or even a boy friend, yet. Do you have a boy friend?"

"Of course, I don't. You would be the first to know. What about you? I've noticed that you and that brainy Ronny Kirkland still manage to put your heads together in study hall."

Amelia looked surprised. "You know darn well, we are

just good friends. He is about the only person in school that seems to know what he is talking about. Too bad, that once he gets out into the real world he crawls into his shell. Nice guy, though. So anyway, why of all things, should I buy my best woman friend a bra for Christmas?"

Trish looked clearly frustrated. "Who else is going to buy it for me? Certainly, not my mother! She still thinks I should be dressing along the lines of *OshKosh!*"

It amazed Amelia that as clever as Trish could be, she often missed the obvious. With some discomfort, she wondered if she could be guilty of the same thing. "Trish, why don't you just buy the bra for yourself?"

"Well, first of all that would not be any fun. Besides what happens in ten years when I'm old, married with a couple of kids, and no one remembers or cares when I got my first push up bra? Wouldn't you want your best friend to share that momentous occasion with you? In fact, that metal cleaner was only a couple of bucks, why don't you look around for something for yourself. I could put that toward your Christmas gift."

"I'm just not in the mood right now. Besides, my mom has already bought me a lot of those things; though, I dare say, not an up lift bra. Anyway, you go ahead and pick out the one that you like, and I will be glad to share the experience with you."

"Do you mean to tell me that Karen has actually recognized that Melie is no longer a child, and that she has blossomed into a young, woman."

Forcing herself to lighten up, Amelia removed a half slip from the rack and covered the lower part of her face, while her eyes glared in Trish's direction. Just as quickly, she returned the slip to its waiting niche. "Trish, I have to hand it to you, you are the only person who makes me feel young again."

"Oh, Melie, that is a bunch of hooey! You were always an old soul, though in the past you were certainly more fun loving. I can only hope that when you return to your old self, you will buy a truck load of these honeys."

"Trish, I love you too."

*　　*　　*　　*

The Pumpkin House was mobbed with Christmas shoppers. Amelia and Trish skidded to a stop in front of the large mahogany doors. "It is a quarter after one, I hope Mom and Granny Lou have already been seated or we are going to have a heck of a wait." With determination, Amelia pulled Trish through the crowd and into the restaurant.

Immediately, the girls were confronted by a less than merry maitre d. "Ah, young ladies you can't just go into the restaurant. Please return to the line outside and wait your turn."

Amelia, spoke up quickly before Trish could open her mouth. She never knew what might follow. "Sir, we believe my mother and grandmother may have already been seated and may be waiting for us. Could we please just take a peek in the dining area to see if they have been seated?"

"Oh, yes, do forgive me; you must be at the Morelli table. Is that correct?"

Both the girls nodded their heads. With considerable relief, they followed the maitre d to the table.

"There you are, and only with a few packages. What on earth were you two doing the entire morning?"

"Sorry, we are late, Mom, but we just lost track of time. Speaking of packages, you don't appear to have many packages either."

Granny Lou immediately came to Karen's defense. "Well Amelia, your mother had the foresight to take our packages to the car before coming back to the restaurant. But that's not really important, let's just order and have a nice lunch, shall we?"

Trish sat down first. "That sounds good, thank you. I am famished."

Granny Lou continued. "Amelia, now sit down next to Trish and tell us about your morning."

"Well, there's nothing to really tell, a lot of people, a lot of stuff. Trish and I managed to get a few things, in fact Trish… Ouch, Trish did you just kick me?"

Trish rolled her eyes. "Now, why would I kick you, Melie?"

While Karen looked perplexed, Granny Lou looked seriously amused. "Have you girls had a shot of catnip or something stronger this morning?"

Karen interjected with affected exuberance. "Isn't the Christmas season wonderful? I've always loved Christmas. Don't you agree, girls?"

Trish concurred. "Oh, yes, Mrs. Morelli, Christmas will always be my most favorite time of the year. I love everything about it, going to church with my family, the excitement, and boy do I love the presents."

Everyone chuckled at Trish's childlike delight. At the same time, Amelia sensed that the focus of the conversation now rested with her. Her dilemma was clear, did she scream at the top of her lungs that she hated Christmas. That neither the presents nor the merriment, the lofty sermons nor angelic hymns, not even her loving family and friends, could make for a happy Christmas without her dad. Amelia lifted her sad eyes and said nothing.

CHAPTER 13

The Invitation

Lou worked for over an hour at drafting a letter to Elizabeth Gale Bissett. Finally satisfied, she pressed the print key on her computer. "Good, I think this accurately explains our plight."

Mike, who had settled into his favorite leather chair across from his wife, looked up from the daily paper. "Did you say something, Lou?"

"Oh, nothing dear, I just finished up my letter to Mrs. Bissett."

Mike looked thoughtful. "Bissett, you know I have heard that name before, something to do with Virginia politics. Oh, yes, it's Gerald Bissett, an up and coming junior senator from Virginia. Possibly, he is Elizabeth's son or grandson; but I guess that is not particularly relevant to the genealogy search."

Lou arched her eyebrows. "That certainly is not a surprise; you are talking about the blue bloods of Virginia society. I would suspect the family has been influential in both local and national politics for generations."

"My, my, I did not realize when I married a Ms. Louise

Amelia Thomas that she came with pedigree papers!" Mike quipped.

"Okay, out of here! I need to get down to business and get this letter in the mail. Hopefully, Mrs. Bissett will take the bait and invite Amelia and me to Galynn Hall. As a good will gesture, I plan to include a copy of my latest book, *Life on Noah's Ark.* Just maybe that will add to my credibility." Lou playfully ushered her husband out of the study.

*　　*　　*　　*

Christmas and New Years day came and went. Amelia maintained the same somber demeanor adopted soon after her father's death. She alone knew of the sinister tricks her mind would unexpectedly play on her. At those times, dark thoughts would steal away from her any capacity for peace or joy. How lost she felt when facing the accuser of her soul, the one who whispered that she alone had been responsible for her father's annihilation.

At her worse, Amelia added her mother's anguish to her repertoire of guilt. This holiday season, she had watched her mother experience higher highs and lower lows, than she had during the first Christmas without her husband. Almost as though the synapses of her mother's brain once mercifully anesthetized from the pain, now lay raw to its sting.

By now, Amelia knew that any magical thinking that her father might walk through the door had ceased for both herself and her mother. When forced to face the finality of her loss, the thought nearly drained the very life from her. In those moments of deep despair, she would pray as hard as she could that what she had learned years earlier in Sunday school would someday come to pass. Only in that reality, would her family ever be reunited.

*　　*　　*　　*

The old adage, *Time heals all.*, continued to stick in Lou's craw. Ironically, that same adage had become the impetus for her continued efforts to help her granddaughter. Though, she maintained the outward appearance of the proverbial optimist, inwardly she fretted as to whether Mrs. Bissett would answer her letter. She continued to play devil's advocate with herself. At times, she imagined Mrs. Bissett throwing her letter into the trash in an attempt to rid herself of an apparent crackpot, who was merely interested in passing herself off as a lost relative.

Continuing to second guess herself, she wondered if what she had shared concerning her granddaughter's recent loss might be misconstrued as a ploy to evoke sympathy for the purpose of gaining an invitation. Fortunately, Lou's pragmatism would save her from herself. She realized that had the woman suspected the worse, she had both the means and resources to look into the matter before choosing to respond. Dr. Beale's blessings added to her security, as had her conviction that Amelia continued to respond positively to her improvisational therapy. These reassurances helped her endure the endless days of suspenseful waiting.

Lou never shared her torturous thoughts with her family, least of all with Amelia. Throughout the long wait, she would think how ironic that Amelia never seemed to doubt that she and her Granny Lou would someday visit at Galynn Hall and meet Elizabeth Gale Bissett. Her granddaughter gave every indication, that for her, it was simply a matter of when their invitation would arrive.

On February 28th, Lou received the response letter she had hoped for. She was jubilant! The letter was handwritten and had been mailed from St. Croix, Virgin Islands. Mrs. Bissett began her letter by explaining why the mistress of Galynn Hall was writing from St. Croix. Apparently, she and family members spent the winter months on the family's sugar cane plantation. At seventy-one years of age, her arthritis was considerably less troublesome in the warmth of the St. Croix sun.

She thanked Lou for sending her a copy of her latest book,

graciously relating how she had spent pleasant afternoons reading to visiting great-grandchildren. Midway into the letter, Mrs. Bissett stated that she would be returning to Galynn Hall, in mid-March. It would be at that time, when she would be only too happy to arrange for a meeting. The letter ended with the hope that she would be able to shed some light upon the Amelia Currick Gale mystery; though Mrs. Bissett refrained from sharing any information she might already have. In conclusion, she provided her private telephone number and requested that Lou contact her during the week of March 20, 2003. She signed her letter, Beth.

"Yes, thank you Beth!" Lou thought it strange to address the mistress of Galynn Hall, as simply, Beth.

Following Beth's favorable response, Lou felt comfortable in putting aside any doubts she might have had. For the moment she was dizzy with excitement, and only wished for someone in the house to share her news with. To think she and Amelia were actually going to walk the estate grounds where one of the family matriarchs had been raised as a child. She relished the thought of finally telling Amelia her wonderful news.

By late afternoon, Lou decided she would share her news that same evening, with the entire family. She called Mike at work and asked him to meet her at their daughter's home after closing. Then with letter in hand, Lou grabbed her purse and overcoat, locked up the house and began the twenty minute drive to her daughter's home. While driving, she dialed up her daughter's phone number. Her eyes danced when she heard Amelia's voice. "Have I got a surprise for you; I'm coming right over! With this traffic I should be at your front door in about thirty minutes. Okay, bye."

Lou found Amelia waiting at the front door. Buoyantly, she bounced out of the car and breezed through the front door like a Midwest twister. "Hold out your hands, palms up!"

Triumphantly, she placed the letter in her granddaughter's opened hands. "Read that, my dear!"

With a knowing look, Amelia opened the letter and began to read. When finished reading, she lifted her head. "Sorry, Granny Lou, but no surprises here. I had no doubt we would be going to Galynn Hall. Who would turn down the opportunity to meet one of the best known children's authors in the country?"

Lou felt flattered, as well as disappointed. "Well, I wish I had been so sure we would receive an invitation. Aren't you the least bit surprised, or how about excited?"

Amelia thought for a moment. "Well, of course I am excited."

Lou motioned Amelia to the couch. "Okay, excited is good! Now, while we wait for your mother and granddad to get here, let's go over the family tree one more time."

"Is Granddad coming here, too?"

"Yes, I thought he would like to help us celebrate. Now, let's go over our family tree." With deliberation, Lou began the oral review. "Well here they are, these are the Thomas women for whom you were named. The only remaining question is whether Amelia Currick Gale is the first, with whom you share your given name. We know for a fact that she married Edan Thomas in 1867, bearing him two sons, my Great-Grandfather Currick Thomas in 1869, and Keegan Edan Thomas in 1871. Keegan never married, and as far as anyone knows never fathered a child. Currick Thomas did marry and fathered three children. They were named Nolan, Amelia, and Peter. Amelia Thomas died of influenza as a child, while the Peter Thomas line did not continue with the use of the name Amelia. Though, my Grandfather Nolan and his wife Katherine Ferguson did continue its use. Their children were named, Leslie Nolan Thomas, Amelia Jane Thomas, and Neil Thomas. We know that my Aunt Mia, short for Amelia, was the mother of a daughter. Aunt Mia was also a respected elementary school teacher for thirty-five years. Neither she nor her daughter, continued with the use of her given name. My father, Leslie Nolan Thomas, named my brother William Leslie Thomas, and of course, I was named Louise Amelia Thomas. My brother, William, had only two sons, and no grandchildren. Of course, I named your mother, Karen. To date, you my dear are the last blood relative to carry the family name. In summary, we know where we end up, but still are not certain where we began. What a mouth full!"

Amelia stared at the Ancestral Chart, while Lou continued. "Look at me, going on this way; why don't you tell me something about you. At the risk of prying, I would love to know what is happening in my granddaughter's life."

"Well, if it were anyone else asking the questions, I would say yes, you are prying." In an attempt to reassure her grandmother, Amelia gave her an unexpected hug. "Anyway, my school life is not as interesting as you might think. I go to school, come home and study and repeat the same thing the next day. But my grades are good!"

Though, Lou thought better of it, she continued with her questions. "What about all those activities you use to be involved in, the music club, student council, and all the friends you use to pal around with? I know I might be off limits, but have you played your piano at all?"

"No, to all of the above; everything makes me sad. Well, except, you already know, I hang out with Trish." Now sullen, Amelia sank back into the generously cushioned chair she occupied.

For a moment, Lou just looked at Amelia, thinking how strange that only a year and a half ago, the family had waited in this same room, for word on her father's fate. "Amelia, please understand, it is okay to feel sad and angry. Life will always give us reasons for both happy and sad feelings. We all have to face our sad feelings head on, so they do not destroy us." Amelia continued to sink deeper into her chair, and Lou was acutely aware that she had pushed the issue far enough. Not wanting to further compromise the festive mood, she stopped speaking.

The grinding sound of the garage door opening, gave Lou the perfect excuse to extricate herself from the mounting tension between herself and Amelia. "Oh, that must be your mom, let me see if I can help her with anything!"

Karen looked weighted down by the oversized tote bag wrapped about her shoulder. "Mom, how nice, what is the occasion?" A look of relief spread across the petit woman's face as she deposited several books onto the kitchen table.

Lou grinned like a Cheshire cat. "Why don't you let me help you find a home for all those books? It looks as though you have emptied the library." Lou's eyes zoomed from the books to her daughter's svelte body. "Karen, you really look quite well; but we are going to have to try and help you gain back some of that much needed weight you have lost."

"Mom, I don't look much different than I had the last time you saw me. Besides, my weight, in due time, will take care of itself. Now, why the broad grin, what's going on?"

Lou chirped. "I just shared the most stupendous news with Amelia."

Before Karen could question her mother further, Amelia marched triumphantly into the kitchen with letter in hand. Amelia repeated for her mother that she had little doubt that she and Granny Lou would be invited to Galynn Hall.

Karen led the way back into the den. "Now, please stop gabbing and let me read this letter."

Karen's mouth curved up into a broad smile. "This is wonderful, it sounds like you are well on your way to solving the Amelia Currick Gale mystery. All you have to do is be patient until Mrs. Bissett returns to Richmond."

The conversation stopped when Mike poked his head into the den. "What a busy day. There seems to be an epidemic of just about everything going around; I can't remember when I have filled so many prescriptions. Well, I guess, I can't complain, business is good! Now, what about this letter? I suppose I'm the last to read Mrs. Bissett's life changing words!"

"I'm afraid so, dear." Lou predictably kissed her husband on the cheek, while Karen immediately left her chair and gave her father a big hug. Amelia hung back, as though hiding within the safety of her chair.

Mike pouted as he leaned over Amelia. "I will read this letter only after I get my kiss." Demurely, Amelia planted a peck in the middle of her granddad's graying hairline.

"That's better! Now let me read this letter everyone is fussing about." After reading the letter Mike removed his bifocals and quipped. "Well it looks like I will be eating alone sometime in the near future. But not tonight, how about in celebration of the good news, I take my favorite girls to dinner at the Le Petit Café?"

Lou anticipated Mike's invitation, and was happy to accept. Karen readily agreed, while Amelia remained quiet.

Mike frowned. "This decision has to be unanimous, what do you say Amelia?" Lou was glad that Mike was not about to allow his granddaughter to shrink back into her protective shell, without some resistance on his part.

"Granddad, I would prefer to celebrate at the Constantine Restaurant." Amelia's tone was uncommonly decisive.

For what seemed an eternity, the room fell silent. Everyone knew full well that Karen and Ken had often eaten at the family run restaurant prior to and after Amelia's birth. Mike dropped his eyes and responded. "But of course, how could I have forgotten that my granddaughter's favorite food is Italian. Karen, is that alright with you?"

Without hesitation, Karen replied. "Sure, Constantine it is!"

*　　*　　*　　*

Little had changed at Constantine's. The greeting was warm and friendly, while the aroma of homemade pasta permeated every alcove of the establishment. Phillip, one of the Constantine sons, seated the family. *"Oh Sig.ra Morelli and giovane donna,* I have not seen you in such a long time. Please come, I will seat you at one of our best tables."

Not long after the family's order had been taken, the food began to be served. The table overflowed with many of the family's favorite dishes, culinary delights deserving of a discerning gastronome. No option remained, but to savor the meal. Karen, whose appetite had waned since her husband's death, ate heartily. Though Amelia selected her dishes, slowly and deliberately, she appeared to relish her food, as well.

Throughout the meal, niceties were exchanged between Phillip and the family. Only after dinner was finished, and the family prepared to leave the restaurant, was any mention made of Ken. Phillip gregariously directed his remark to Karen. "Say hello to *il mio amico intelligente!"* Karen lowered her eyes, though she remained smiling. The rest of the family continued their walk to the car, while Karen remained behind. Discreetly, she pulled Phillip out of hearing range of other patrons. "Phillip, I'm sorry to share very sad news with you, but Ken was one of the fatalities in the attack upon the World Trade Center."

Tears welled up in both Karen and Phillip's eyes. Visibly shaken, Phillip spoke. *"Oh Sig.ra Morelli,* please forgive me, I did not know. My deceased father and Frank Morelli were friends from the old country; my family can do nothing less than offer up a Requiem mass for his eldest son. Oh, I am so very sorry!"

Though her heart pounded, Karen tried to reassure Phillip. "Phillip, it is all right, I'm sorry your family had not been notified. Thank you for offering your prays in Ken's name; he would be pleased. Now, you take care, dear friend." Karen hugged the trembling man and closed the door behind her.

*   *   *   *

The family pensively awaited Karen's return to the car. Lou's face etched in concern for her daughter, tried to remain calm as she turned to Amelia. "Amelia, what did the waiter say to your mother?"

"Well, because the Constantine brothers knew my dad was a Yale graduate, who spoke fluent Italian, they always called him their smart friend. Phillip said to say hello, to his smart friend."

Lou hoped neither Amelia nor Mike caught the quiver of her lower lip. Gently she continued to question Amelia. "Honey, did you have a reason for choosing the Constantine Restaurant, other than the delicious Italian food?"

In a barely audible voice, Amelia answered her grandmother. "I just wanted Dad to be a part of the celebration."

THOMAS FAMILY TREE (FROM 1833 TO PRESENT)

Edan Thomas 1833-1895
Married
Amelia Currick Gate 1844-1918

Currick Edan Thomas 1869-1941
Married
Abigail Bridge 1872-1922

Keegan Thomas 1871-1901
Unmarried, no children

Nolan Thomas 1897-1959
Married
Katherine Ferguson 1896-1962

Aurelia Thomas
1900-1903

Peter Thomas 1902-1983
Married
Hedy Smith 1906-1956

Leslie Nolan Thomas 1920-1989
Married
Louise Johnsen 1922-2000

Amelia Jane Thomas 1921-
Married
Fred Roth 1915-1999

Neal Thomas 1923-2002
Married
Constance Arthur 1923-1958

Peter Smith Thomas 1924-2001
Married no children
Susan Morris 1923-1999

Henry Thomas 1926-1998
Married
Natalie Dupre 1930-

(Children from the fourth and future generations indicated on following pages.)

Leslie Nolan Thomas 1920-1989
Married
Louise Johnson 1922-2000

William Leslie Thomas 1940-
Married
April Holt 1944-

Louise Amelia Thomas 1941-
Married
Michael McDowell 1936-

William Leslie Thomas, Jr. 1971-
Married, no children
Elizabeth Stewart 1975-

Walter Nolan Thomas 1978-
Unmarried, no children

Alex Michel McDowell 1961-
Married
Patricia Van Ness 1964-

Karen McDowell 1963-
Married
Kenneth Frank Morelli 1963-2001

Mathew McDowell 1982-
Unmarried, no children

Andrew McDowel 1984-

Amelia Morelli 1987-

Amelia Jane Thomas 1921–
Married
Fred Roth 1915-2000

Katherine Roth 1945-
Married
Christopher Bowman 1940-

Christopher Bowman, Jr. 1977-
Unmarried, no children

Neal Thomas 1923-2002
Married, no children
Constance Arthur 1923-1958

Peter Smith Thomas 1924-2001
Married
Susan Morris 1923-1999

Susan Carol Thomas 1954-
Married
Carl Baumgartner 1950-

Peter Smith Thomas, Jr. 1957-
Married
Jennifer Lassiter 1960-

Katlyn Baumgartner 1980-

Lavina Baumgartner 1985-
Unmarried no children

Colson Peter Thomas 1985-

Perry Smith Thomas 1990-

Henry Thomas 1926-1998
Married
Natalie Dupre 1930-

Barry Henry Thomas 1955-
Married
Joanne Hizaemias 1965-

Nicole Laine Thomas 1965-
Married
Roger Ridgeway 1963-

Henry Adrian Thomas 2000-

Natalie Nicole Ridgeway 2001-

CHAPTER 14

Galynn Hall

Following the receipt of Mrs. Bissett's letter, Amelia lived vicariously through her grandmother. The raw excitement she would not yet permit herself to feel, oozed from her grandmother's every pore. Amelia wondered how a grown woman could become so captivated by the mystery surrounding a woman she had never known. Only when she dared be honest with herself, did she realized her own fascination with her namesake.

Sometimes, Amelia would fantasize about Amelia Currick Gale and her father. She would imagine that they had met in some faraway realm. Possibly, she thought, the lady might have confided in her father. Just maybe, he knew the matriarch's secret, as well as her own.

It would be March 24th, before Amelia would receive more news from her grandmother. She learned that her Granny Lou, with considerable trepidation, had placed a phone call to Elizabeth Gale Bissett. With great pleasure, and without hesitation, she accepted an invitation for herself and Amelia to visit Galynn Hall on April 10th.

"Granny Lou, you are amazing, not only do we have an invitation, but April 10th is during my Spring break. My good grades are about the only thing Mom seems happy about lately; she will be pleased that I will not be missing any time from my studies."

*   *   *   *

Lou's mind raced fast forward with plans to make the four hundred forty six mile drive to Charles City, Virginia. Situated some eighteen miles east of Richmond, Galynn Hall was one of several stately plantation homes lining the scenic banks of the James River. Earlier research indicated that the area was well known for its eighteenth century homes. In light of the historical nature of the homes, many had been open to the public. Consequently, the area had become a popular tourist attraction.

The morning of April 9th was a flurry of activity. Taking no chances on over sleeping, Lou set her alarm clock for 5:00 AM. Though, on this morning she had little reason to believe she would not rise by the crack of dawn. Amelia, over the past year, had become very different in this regard. Lou felt it prudent to have the girl sleep over the night before their scheduled departure in order to avert any delay.

The aroma of fresh brewed coffee quickened Lou's step as she made her way down the stairs and into the kitchen. To her surprise, Amelia stood waiting for her. The sixteen year old was dressed, packed and ready to begin the journey. Always thoughtful, Amelia had prepared coffee and a light breakfast of cold cereal for both herself and her grandparents.

"Well, aren't you the early one; I hope I am not holding you up!" Lou beamed as she spoke to her lovely granddaughter.

Flippantly, Amelia retorted. "Why, not at all, Granny Lou. Why would you think I would be in a hurry on the dawn of my vacation?"

Lou laughed, and instinctively patted Amelia on her form fitting jean clad derriere. "That's my old Amelia!"

Without haste they downed a bowl of cereal and a cup of Amelia's enticing coffee. As they gulped their last drop of brew, a sleepy Mike lumbered into the kitchen. "Well, it looks as though the travelers are about ready to go. Weren't you going to share a cup of Java with me before you left?"

"Here, dear. Amelia brewed the coffee and it is delicious. Of course, we would not have left without feeding you and saying goodbye. Now, eat your breakfast and then if you would, help us put our luggage in the back of the SUV." Lou, teasingly throw her husband a kiss.

Mike pointed to his cup of coffee. "This nectar of the gods will keep me going for the time being. Let's get you two on the road." Mike grabbed two of the three suitcases from the hallway, while Lou managed the last piece of luggage. Together they marched toward the detached garage.

The air was cold and brisk, a typical early spring, New England morning. Lou and Amelia were both prepared; a bulky pullover was the last piece of clothing over their layered attire. Mike, on the other hand, stood shivering in his pajamas and old red flannel shirt. Lou chastised herself. "Oh Mike, I should not have asked for your help, you will catch your death of cold."

"I would not miss the opportunity to escort two beautiful women to their vehicle. Which, you will be pleased to know, was given a clean bill of health. Your chariot is gassed and ready to go. Now, all you have to do is drive carefully. Let me know when you reach your destination."

"Thank you for looking after us; we will be careful. There are four ready to- go- dinners in the freezer. If you get lonely, Karen would love your company. Well, we better get on our way; love you dear." The three hugged and said goodbye.

Lou and Amelia smiled at one another, both glad to be on the road. Lou remained hopeful that by the journey's end they would have successfully solved the Amelia Currick Gale mystery. She also believed that the long drive might be an excellent opportunity to gain further insight into Amelia's apparent struggles. Though, past conversation with her granddaughter, left Lou acutely aware that unwelcomed probing would be counterproductive.

The sun made its appearance on the horizon, with the promise of a clear spring day. Lou navigated the George Washington Bridge, followed by the Whitestone Bridge, taking them well on their way toward I-95. Within two hours of driving they approached the two hour stretch of the Jersey Turnpike. Lou thought this would be the perfect time to update Amelia on Matt's latest information.

She gave Amelia a gentle tap with her elbow. The teenager sat adorned in headphones, lost to one of the CDs, Lou had the foresight to bring on the trip. With obvious reluctance, Amelia removed the headphones and looked at her grandmother with questioning eyes.

Lou met Amelia's gaze and answered her unspoken question. "I thought you might be interested in the latest information Matt has come up with." Before waiting for Amelia's response she continued. "It seems the Winfield 67 acre family farm is located all but a few miles from Galynn Hall."

Amelia perked up. "Well that is curious, how do you suppose a family whose ancestors had been slaves would end up owning prime real estate just adjacent to Galynn Hall? Also, I thought there had been speculation that Mazzie Winfield had in some way been involved in Amelia Currick Gale's disappearance? Sounds like another mystery, Granny Lou."

Lou smiled. "It gets even better; the land now known as Winfield Farm was actually part of the original 684 acres surrounding Galynn Hall. According to the 1872 property tax records, a 342 acre parcel of land had been placed into Pearl Winfield's hands soon after Justin Gale inherited the estate. Apparently, Pearl was Mazzie's mother."

I've read in my history books that following the end of the Civil War, slave owners, out of guilt or attachment, would provide their slaves with homesteads. It almost seems like the decent thing to do, considering the blacks had served white families for generations without compensation. Sort of, like reparations. Still, in this case, why so many acres to Pearl Winfield?" Amelia grimaced and took a deep breath.

"I don't know, dear. Hopefully, this will all be cleared up when we speak with Beth. Are you enjoying the music your old granny selected for your entertainment?"

"Well, your musical taste certainly runs the gamut, from Mozart to the Goldfish Boys. Too bad Lilly isn't here, she has a mammoth crush on the Goldfish's lead singer. Or, at least she did."

Lou was quick to recognize the bridge which would help her to once again broach the family's loaded question. "While we are on the topic of music…" Before she could complete her sentence, Amelia uncharacteristically interrupted. "Please, Granny Lou; I do not wish to discuss the piano!"

Lou quickly backed away from her question. She felt both clumsy and pushy, something she rarely experienced when speaking her mind to Amelia. "Alright Amelia, I will respect your wishes. Now, please, let's just enjoy the rest of our time together, shall we?"

"Yes, of course, Granny Lou." Amelia reassuringly stroked her grandmother's right shoulder.

The rest of the trip proved uneventful. A packed lunch was consumed during the drive, with only one stop to refuel and visit the restroom. Within nine hours of beginning the journey, the travelers pulled into the parking lot of the Hilton River View. The hotel was situated between Richmond and Charles City, and had been selected for its close proximity to Galynn Hall. The plan was to live out of the hotel until completion of their business.

When the travelers reached their room they unpacked and

then leisurely ate a quiet dinner within the hotel restaurant. Both were fatigued, and sleep that night came swiftly. Even the anticipated early morning breakfast with Beth at Galynn Hall, did not interfere with their slumber.

*　　*　　*　　*

With the new dawn, Amelia once again took satisfaction in surprising Lou by rising early. Somehow, she had managed to dress and complete her toiletry before the 7:00 AM screech of the bedside clock. Lou, on the other hand, overslept and was jolted into wakefulness by the clock's alarm.

Teasingly, Lou squinted and then spoke. "Well, aren't you turning into a predictable creature of the morning light."

"Granny Lou, you forget all the years I was up at 5:00 AM to practice the piano, well before the start of school." It was hard to miss the scolding tone of Amelia's voice.

"No disputing that, Amelia! No one, including myself, really gave it too much thought. We all felt that you loved to play the piano so very much."

Amelia looked thoughtful. "Well, I did! I guess you better get yourself together or we will be late for our appointment with Mrs. Bissett, or is it Beth? Have you tried to imagine what she is like?"

"I'm certain she is as gracious as her letter and telephone persona suggest. We will know for sure, very soon. Well, any way, once again you are right, I had better get myself together. I think I will take a quick shower." Lou stepped into the bathroom, closing the door behind her.

*　　*　　*　　*

The drive along the John Tyler Highway, magically transported Amelia back to a time, she now struggled to understand. Her keen imagination allowed her to envision the family matriarch as a young girl frolicking through the surrounding woods. Only the infrequent appearance of another vehicle or a random service station returned her to the twenty-first century. Well into the drive, she had caught glimpses of the dozen or more stately hilltop manor homes dotting the panoramic view. Closer to the road, stone walls stood sentinel over the manor homes. She laughed to herself, what threat could possibly warrant those sturdy walls? Could the interloper be the James River, which throughout the ride had played hide and seek with the asphalt road. Always with practiced stealth the river would remain hidden save for the parting of the lush spring foliage.

A short distance into the drive, Lou made a sharp right turn into the entrance of Galynn Hall. Amelia looked upward some fifteen feet above the drive, at the gray stone support columns. As far as she could see, the property remained enclosed to itself by antique bronze and wrought iron fencing almost as high as the gates. The entrance promised a structure of strength and solitude. True to its promise, Galynn Hall had never been opened to the public as had many of the other area plantations.

A few yards in front of the elaborate gate, situated in the middle of the two lane entrance, stood a more than adequate stone gatehouse. Lou opened her window and communicated their arrival to the polite yet formal gatekeeper. With the press of a button, the gates electronically opened, allowing the visitors to continue their drive toward the manor house. Out of earshot of the gatekeeper, Lou joked with Amelia. "This must be like dying and entering the pearly gates. The only change I would ask is that the reception be a mite more welcoming. I would be worried if this were the real thing!"

Amelia listened to the foreign sound her own laughter. "Granny Lou stop clowning around, I don't want to arrive at Mrs. Bissett's door chuckling like an immature idiot."

"Well, it is good to hear you laugh again; but if I must, I will get serious. Just look at this beautiful place!"

The remaining one mile drive to the main house boasted

a kaleidoscope of indigenous flowering plants. An array of Daffodils, Redbud trees and Forsythia welcomed the visitors. Boldly the vivid sea of color flowed throughout the wood line, gracing the entire landscape.

Surrounded by an oasis of green, the manor house rested at the pinnacle of the long driveway. Then, in an indeterminable distance, the green lawn merged with impressionistic flair with the blue waters of the James River. It was here that the pastoral scene completed itself.

The size of the magnificent Galynn Hall was further accentuated by its hilltop elevation, which was considerable for the relatively flat terrain of the Virginia tidewater region. By way of a recently constructed circular drive, arriving vehicles were placed immediately at the front entrance of the mansion. Three steps from the gravel roadway led to a two-tiered portico, upon which sat a third level. The portico was supported by bold white pillars with elaborate woodwork, further accentuating the massiveness of the building's midsection. On either side, the midsection stood symmetrically flanked by two story wings. In their entirety, the wings were constructed of the same gray stone used to build the gate columns. The crowning glory of the structure was its French Mansard roof with large, prominent dormers.

Neither Lou nor Amelia, were strangers to wealth and privilege, their relation to the well heeled Morelli family, being no exception. Still, not even their comfortable middle class lifestyle, nor their extensive historical review of the area, had prepared them for Galynn Hall's display of enduring opulence.

With resolve, Lou pushed forward. "Well Amelia, are you ready to meet Elizabeth Gale Bissett?"

Amelia kept her enthusiasm in check, though she was ever so ready to meet the mistress of such a grand old house. Nonchalantly, she shrugged her shoulders. "Let's go!"

Together, they stepped from the SUV and made their

approach toward the looming double oak doors. Before Lou's hand found the door knocker, the right side of the door opened. A stately woman, who appeared to be in her early sixties, greeted them. Her silver white hair was worn in a short layered cut which flattered her distinctly square face.

Amelia hung back as her grandmother skillfully interacted with the pleasant woman. Before introductions were made, she watched as both women discretely scrutinized one another. Amelia was certain her grandmother had noticed the woman's flawless complexion, which then gave accent to her soft blue eyes. Lean and tall, she wore a plain light blue paisley frock, with flat loafers. Only after she extended her crippled hand in welcome, did Amelia catch the glint of knowing in her grandmother's eyes. This was none other than Elizabeth Gale Bissett.

At the invitation of their hostess, Lou and Amelia entered a large open atrium. Elizabeth's welcome of the two strangers continued with an unassuming grace that only true humility seasoned with years of practice could have perfected. "Oh, how foolish of me for not introducing myself, I am Elizabeth Bissett, please call me Beth. Lou, it is a delight to finally meet you. I have been looking forward to this for months. Amelia, your grandmother was modest in describing you, such a ravishingly beautiful young woman."

Amelia simultaneously blushed and smiled; hating herself for behaving like a self conscious schoolgirl. Fortunately, her Granny Lou remembered her manners and thanked Beth for her kind words. It was at this point, that Amelia with considerable relief decided that she would follow her grandmother's lead, as she interviewed Beth. Needless to say, she knew from first impression that Beth was no less skilled than her grandmother in the art of communication, and certainly had an agenda of her own.

*　　*　　*　　*

Beth motioned her guests to follow her. "Come, I have breakfast waiting for us in the sun room." Together the three women walked through the atrium. Lou and Amelia marveled at the graceful semi-circular stairway with steps on either side of the atrium. As the staircase climbed, its 15 foot bridge formed the floor of the second story. Hanging from the atrium's 30 foot ceiling and centered immediately above the women, was a bedazzling blue crystal chandelier. Beneath the chandelier, from front to rear, the atrium remained free of pillars or walls. As guests made their way toward the sun room, the openness of the atrium allowed for an unobstructed view of the James River.

The sun room was located through the last door on the left side of the atrium. The visitors entered the room to find wall to wall French windows and doors, giving access to a back veranda, as well as continuation of the panoramic view. Lured by the aroma of steaming hot breakfast foods kept warm on stainless steel burners, Lou and Amelia turned their attention away from the visual delights of the surroundings.

"Please sit down, will you? I'm sure you will enjoy a good breakfast after yesterday's long day of travel." Beth motioned her guest toward the meticulously prepared table. "Since the topic of our conversation is of a personal nature, the servers have been instructed that we are not to be interrupted. I hope you do not mind that we are on our own, actually I prefer it that way."

Lou and Amelia were fast to support Beth's decision.

When satisfied that her guests had had ample food, Beth turned the conversation to the business at hand. "Now, tell me, could I possibly claim you lovely ladies as kin?" Beth stopped, and Lou picked up on the cue, furnishing Beth with added details of their plight. Beth listened intently, while Amelia remained silent.

"Well, that is very interesting to say the least." Beth raised her eyebrows as she spoke. "Let me show you what I have gathered up these past few days in anticipation of your visit." Beth walked toward an antique cherry wood cabinet, standing in the back of the room. She opened a large drawer removing a green velvet covered box and an oversized blue satin covered diary. Inside the box were several documents as well as numerous pre-civil war photos. One by one, Beth removed these items, careful to place them onto the clean end of the dining table.

"Well, this should help answer some of your questions, though I am afraid not all of them. My parents, many years ago during a home renovation stumbled upon the treasures I am about to share with you. During the Civil War, in an attempt to keep family valuables out of the hands of union soldiers, items of either personal or monetary worth were hidden. Within Galynn Hall, a back stairway leading to an obscure room, served as a hiding place. Ransacked many times during the occupation, objects made of gold and silver were stolen, while items such as books were left behind in disarray. When my parents went through an old armoire, they discovered Adelaide's diary and other memorabilia under a clutter of ragged clothes. Let's take a look at some of the more revealing documents retrieved; starting first with Malin Gale's Last Will and Testament. I believe this to be irrefutable proof that upon his death Malin had wished for his wife, Adelaide, to inherit his entire estate. In the event that Malin would have survived his wife, his wish was for the couple's three children to inherit an equal third of the estate upon his own death. He also stipulated that if any of the three children died before he did, their inheritance would be equally divided amongst the surviving siblings."

Lou and Amelia carefully handled the fragile document. Lou began mulling over the apparent facts. It would seem likely that Beth knew that Everton had been killed in the Civil War and in all probability she knew Adelaide's fate as well. Only upon the assumption that the entire Gale family, with the exception of Justin, had died, would it seem plausible that Justin Gale would have been the sole beneficiary of the estate. Nothing Beth had shared, explained the Amelia Currick Gale mystery, nor how Pearl Winfield came into possession of 342 acres from the original estate.

With a quizzical expression on her face, Lou looked up from the document. Before she could speak, Beth carefully handed her guest an old yellowed letter as well as a magnifying glass. "I'm sure this is of relevance. The magnifying glass will assist you in deciphering the words written on the fragile paper. The letter had been discreetly folded and tucked away into the seam of Adelaide's diary. It was only through chance that it had been found."

Lou shared the letter with Amelia, and together they read the faded words. When she had finished the letter, Lou looked into Amelia's face. Slowly, Amelia looked up, and in an incredulous whisper, voiced the unexpected truth. "Amelia Currick Gale had been adopted!"

"Yes!" Beth filled in the details. "According to the diary, Adelaide had bemoaned her inability to bear any more children as a consequence of complications in birthing Everton. Though she and Malin had been blessed with two healthy sons, she had longed for a daughter. Information taken from the letter of agreement you just read, as well as from inserts within Adelaide's diary, describe the following circumstances."

"Amelia Currick Gale had been the seventh child of Rourke Currick and his wife Sarah. Rourke had been a tenant farmer working a track of land on the Gale tobacco plantation in Roanoke. Unfortunately, Sarah had died in birthing the child. When the news reached the Gale family, the fate of Sarah's infant had been unknown."

"The Currick family had a long history working the Gale family land. Rourke's father, Aedan Currick, and his mother Finola, had agreed to work as indentured servants on the Roanoke plantation in return for free passage from their native Ireland. The couple labored fifteen hard years before earning their freedom. In the fourth decade of their lives, they continued to work the land as tenant farmers. It was at this time that the couple would be blessed with their only child, a son they named Rourke."

Beth took a breath and continued. "Though the journey from Richmond to Roanoke was long and tedious, nevertheless, Adelaide on occasion would accompany her husband. When she did, she always visited with the Currick family. Rourke had grown into a fine strapping man, and had taken pretty Sarah for his wife. The couple continued to farm the land and have children together. Adelaide had always enjoyed the couple's flaxen haired children. Through the years, she had willingly provided the family with food and other necessities. Needless to say, she was very saddened in learning of Sarah's death. She had had two difficult pregnancies, the second of which brought her close to death. How could the woman not have felt empathy for Sarah, as well as for her child? Adelaide grew insistent that Malin travel with her to the Roanoke plantation so that she might express her condolences and help with the Currick children as best she could. Fortunately, it had been mid September, and snow and ice were of no concern. With the weather taken into account, Malin relented and escorted his wife on her mission."

Lou and Amelia sat mesmerized while Beth continued without interruption. "Well, according to Adelaide's diary, the couple arrived in Roanoke to find the Currick family in dire straits. Fortunately, the Currick's infant daughter had survived the birth. Wonderful as that news was, Rourke of course, was distort over his wife's untimely death as well as the prospect of having to care for another child without her help. Providing for the family over the years had continued to be difficult at best for the young couple. To make matters worse, Rourke's oldest daughter, Cora, was all but seven years old. Hardly mature enough to take full charge of three younger siblings and a newborn infant. The young girl's older brothers were no more than ten and eight years of age."

"Following the Gale's arrival in Roanoke, Malin attended to business, while Adelaide spent her time gathering up food and other supplies. Placing the items into her wagon, she and a farm hand hitched up the horses in preparation for the drive to the Currick homestead. When the wagon pulled up to the Currick porch, Adelaide was greeted by five of the children. Without exception they appeared very unhappy, ill kept, and hungry. Adelaide, soon learned that after burying his wife, Rourke had closed himself off from his children, retreating to the barn for several days. There he sat, without food or comfort, as he grieved for his wife. Neighbors had done what little they could to help. After caring for their own large families, neighboring women who were nursing took turns breastfeeding the frail infant."

"Adelaide's priorities quickly changed when she learned that Sarah's infant had survived. With the children in tow, she made a beeline for the dilapidated shack, which served as the Currick home. Inside, she found Cora despondently rocking the fitful baby, lying in the same cradle, Rourke had carved months earlier. Though alive, the infant was both dehydrated and colicky. Adelaide hugged Cora, and directed her to help herself to the bread and jam, the other children had carried in from the wagon. While the youngsters ate, Adelaide lovingly cradled the fussing infant in her arms. Gently she coaxed the baby to take warm milk from the glass feeding bottle and makeshift nipple she had once used to nurse Everton. To her satisfaction, the infant sucked the bottle dry. Adelaide then swaddled the child in a warm blanket taken from her provisions, and waited for the baby to fall asleep. With ambivalence, she laid the infant back into her cradle and attended to the older children."

Lou was glad when Amelia politely interrupted. "Adelaide must have been a very kind woman!"

Beth stopped her narrative to affirm Amelia's conclusion. "Yes, Amelia she certainly was. If you would like, I will lend you her diary for as long as you remain in the Richmond area. Through reading the diary you will glean an understanding of the family interaction, as well as relevant events. You will find that as well as being kind, Adelaide was also very detail oriented."

Amelia and Lou thanked Beth for her generous offer. Lou felt especially good that their hostess was willing to trust them with an irreplaceable family treasure.

Once again, Beth continued with the family's story. "After cooking up a pot of stew from the fresh foods she had brought with her, Adelaide fed and washed the children. The woman then prepared a bowl of stew for the children's father. With care she carried the nourishment to the barn. She could not help comparing the run down barn with the way she was beginning to feel. With her last ounce of strength, Adelaide opened the dilapidated old door to find Rourke sitting upon a bale of hay. His bleached worn face hung low, and he looked no less dead than his wife. Adelaide moved closer to the large man, then not unlike the way in which she had coaxed his small infant to take the bottle, she gently persuaded him to eat the food she had placed in front of him. In that cold, dark place, Adelaide assured him that she would help as best she could. In the moments that followed, she suggested temporarily taking the weak, colicky infant to the plantation until the child grew stronger. An expression of relief surfaced across Rourke's face, and he readily agreed to the arrangement."

"With the baby secured in her cradle, Adelaide placed her precious cargo in the back of the wagon. For only a moment, she regretted she had not brought one of the house slaves to help her. It was often the case, that her independent streak would override her sound judgment. Fortunately, at the journey's end, she and the infant arrived intact, and her vindication for tending to the family alone, was realized."

"During the weeks that followed Adelaide nursed and loved the nameless child. Any remaining time left to her, was spent helping Rourke Currick and his motherless children assume some sense of normalcy. Within days, Adelaide would develop a strong attachment for the sickly baby. Under her care the child continued to show significant improvement. Though the baby remained fragile, her small cherubic face had begun to fill out and golden hair sprouted atop of her round doll like head."

"Adelaide knew full well that she and Malin would soon have to return to their own children, who remained under Pearl's supervision, at Galynn Hall. As the weeks passed, it became increasingly clear to the couple, that leaving the infant behind was no longer an option. Adelaide was convinced that the only solution would be for her and Malin to adopt the child. Following weeks of discussion, Malin eventually agreed to negotiate an adoption with Rourke. Adelaide justified her decision, in her knowing that should the child be left without constant care, she could easily slip away as her mother had. Malin's sentiments were far different. A shrewd and tough businessman, he had neither the cause nor desire to rear another man's child. The chink in his armor had always been his adored wife, had this not been the case he would have never agreed to the adoption."

"Following the sixth week of Sarah Currick's passing, Rourke was politely summoned to the Gale plantation. When he arrived, Malin was quick to present his proposal. Rourke, though a good man who dearly loved his family, knew his options were limited. If he wanted to keep the rest of his family together, he understood he would be wise to accept the Gale's generous offer. Before agreeing to the arrangement, Rourke soulfully requested of Adelaide that the baby be given the middle name Currick, and be told of her parentage in adult years. In addition, he requested aid in establishing a new homestead in the Smokey Mountains of North Carolina. He explained that kin had settled in that area. Before Adelaide signed the agreement, Malin inked in the added requests. With tears in his eyes, Rourke placed his mark on the agreement, as well."

"In return for allowing the Gales to keep his tiny daughter, Rourke would be allotted $ 10,000.00. Mind you, today this would be equivalent to a quarter of a million dollars. In addition to help with the family's relocation, Rourke was promised the services of a young black woman to care for the children. Malin carefully reviewed the terms of the adoption for Adelaide and Rourke, before signing the document himself."

"As Rourke turned to leave, Adelaide invited him to hold his tiny daughter for the last time. Rourke refused, stating he might change his mind if he did so. Adelaide tried to reassure the distort man that his child was already loved and would be given anything she needed. Before taking his leave, Rourke looked deep into Adelaide's eyes and stated that he believed, other than his beloved Sarah, his child could not have a finer woman to call mother."

"During the long journey back to Galynn Hall, the couple agreed it would be best to pass the infant off as their biological child. Adelaide, having left the Netherlands to become Malin Gale's bride twelve years earlier, painfully remembered how difficult it had been for her to gain the acceptance of Virginia's aristocracy. Though Adelaide had every intention of honoring her promise to Rourke, she did not want the truth of her daughter's parentage to threaten the girl's acceptance, nor jeopardize her prospects of marrying well. She felt more than justified in withholding the truth from her daughter until well after she had made a suitable marriage."

"The Gales also discussed giving their new daughter a proper Christian name. Due to the circumstances of the baby's birth, she had neither been named nor baptized. Malin suggested naming the child Adelaide, in honor of his wife. Adelaide though flattered, thought ill of the idea. She explained that she wanted her daughter to be her own person with her own name. A name befitting the good and beautiful person she knew the baby would grow to become. Seemingly, with little thought at all, Adelaide announced that she wished for the child to be named Amelia. She explained that the name meant hardworking; a characteristic she already credited the small baby with. After all, she explained, the child had to work harder than most just to stay alive. Once again, Adelaide had the last word, as Malin willingly deferred to her wishes."

"Within two months following the couple's return to Richmond, the infant was baptized at the St. James Episcopal Church. Church records show that Amelia Currick Gale had been the child's documented Christian name."

Beth ended her narrative and handed the oversized diary to Amelia. "I have marked pages within the diary which should give you a sense of the personalities within the Gale family. You will find a considerable amount of information about the young girl who would become your ancestral grandmother. She and Adelaide had a very special relationship."

Lou looked at Amelia and pointed at the diary. "That certainly is a lot to digest, don't you think?"

Before Amelia could reply, Beth motioned her guests toward the veranda door. "Please come with me, I believe you will find this of interest." Lou and Amelia dutifully followed Beth through the meticulously tended English garden just below the veranda. Beyond the garden, the women passed a large pond, and Beth mentioned that it had evolved from a natural spring. Softly the spring gurgled from above the surrounding landscape, musically feeding its crystal clear water to the pond below.

Beth's strong, clear voice interrupted the tranquility of the moment. "This spring and pond have been here well before Galynn Hall was constructed in 1744. In fact, the home was named Galynn Hall, reflecting the family surname Gale, combined with lynn, meaning pool below a waterfall. Rather miraculously, it continues to sustain itself."

Lou, who had remained uncharacteristically quiet throughout the visit, commented on Beth's obvious joy when discussing Galynn Hall.

"Yes, I love this place and feel very blessed indeed, that this is my home." As Beth spoke her pace never slowed. It was not long before Lou and Amelia followed their hostess over a stone bridge spanning the narrow end of the pond. Several yards from the bridge lay a parcel of land which served as the family graveyard. There were many headstones, and it appeared as though the area was nearly filled to capacity. Beth moved toward the older gravesites, pointing out the last resting place for both Everton and Justin Gale. Their gravesites were overshadowed by an adjacent seven-foot granite stone. Beth stopped and in silence looked at the monument. The engraving still legible clearly marked the gravesite of Malin and Adelaide Gale.

Malin had lived from March 22, 1809 through February 25, 1870, surviving Adelaide by seven years. Adelaide had been born on February 2, 1815 and died at the age of 48 years on April 13, 1863.

Amelia with tears in her eyes read aloud the tombstone epithet. *"Hearts broken in life, the Almighty surely mends through death."*

Lou's heart sank. "I guess the Gales never did find out what had become of their daughter, had they?" Beth also appeared saddened. "No, judging from the inserts within Adelaide's diary, up to the time of her death the Gales had not learned the fate of their daughter. Unfortunately, soon after the girl's disappearance, Virginia had seceded from the Union. Consequently, most of the Gale family resources and energy was put into supporting the Confederacy."

Beth continued. "The family believed that Adelaide had died of a broken heart. Not only had she lost her only daughter, but she worried over the safety of her two sons. Both Justin and Everton had enlisted in General Lee's Army of Northern Virginia. Needless to say, they were extremely vulnerable for injury or death. It's no wonder that one morning the dear woman never woke from her sleep."

"Justin's memoirs give credence to the presumption, that though Malin had physically survived his wife, he was left a man without a soul. Malin's only consolation seemed to be that his beloved wife did not have to bear the death of their youngest son nor the desecration of the South and its way of life. A way of life, that for even those who would question its sanctity, had nevertheless become accustomed to."

"Well, now I am rambling." Beth shook her head. "Let me just clarify that based upon conjecture, I believe no one in the family had had word concerning what might have happened to Amelia Currick Gale. Though, strangely, following Malin's death, Justin in 1872, had transferred ownership of 342 acres of Gale family land to Pearl Winfield. We have often wondered if there could be a connection between Justin's unorthodox behavior and his sister's disappearance. Lou, with the thorough research you have put into tracking down your forebear, surely you must have come across this puzzling piece of information?"

Lou felt a rush of excitement. "Yes, in fact Amelia and I were discussing those very facts as we drove south to meet with you. We were hoping you would be able to shed light on why this had occurred."

"No, I'm sorry. Justin never left a clue as to the reason for his bizarre behavior. At least nothing I have been able to uncover." Beth openly wore her frustration.

Lou looked thoughtful. "Do you suppose the Winfield family might have information pertaining to the unusual transaction?"

"Well, you certainly can try approaching them. I warn you, even if they do know anything their lips have been sealed for generations. Oh, there is something else which might help you. I know that Mazzie Winfield had returned to the area soon after Pearl had somehow secured the property. If my arithmetic is correct, Mazzie should have been thirty-two years old when she returned to Charles City. Pearl had been ill for sometime, and died a couple years later in 1874. Pearl's sole heir had been Mazzie. Even though the written law had not kept up with the times, Justin made certain that Mazzie inherited what had come to be called Winfield Farm. News clippings state that when questioned by those who remembered the Amelia Currick Gale disappearance, Mazzie flatly denied knowing anything. She claimed no knowledge of what might have happened to her mistress, nor what the woman's current disposition might be. Curiously, once again Justin took Mazzie's part and she remained unscathed. This is about the extent of what I know."

Looking bewildered, Beth shook her head. "When we get back to the house I will give you the telephone number for Dr. Samuel Cotter or Dr. Sam as the locals call him. He is Mazzie's youngest grandson, and now he owns the place."

*   *   *   *

The grand tour ended beneath a wall size mural located within the enormous formal dining area of the mansion. Beth proudly announced. "Now is a good time to place the faces upon our forebears, don't you think? This portrait of the Malin Gale family had been completed not long before Amelia Currick Gale disappeared."

As they walked closer to the mural, Lou noted a look of expectation upon Beth's face. Within seconds of viewing the portrait, Amelia blurted out a truth that no one could refute. "I can't believe the astonishing resemblance between Adelaide and her adopted daughter."

Beth knowingly smiled. "Yes the resemblance is uncanny; the same blond ethereal beauty. When you have a chance to peruse Adelaide's diary, you will find that the likeness went far beyond their appearance. As you might well imagine, the entire family loved Amelia as their own blood. That knowledge only served to make the girl's disappearance all the more mysterious."

Lou and Amelia took notice of Malin, and the couple's two sons, as well. They noted that though Malin had been stockier and shorter in stature than his wife, he had also been an attractive figure. Justin looked very much like his mother, tall, blond and handsome, only resembling his father, in his manly strength. Everton no less attractive, possessed features of both his parents. He had been tall and strong, with darker hair than his brother, and a squared off jaw not unlike his father.

Following the visual introduction to the founding family, it was well into the afternoon. Lou and Amelia were tired and ready to return to the hotel. Beth's graciousness never faltered, she invited her guests to spend the rest of their stay at Galynn Hall. Lou, a firm believer in not wearing out one's welcome, declined Beth's offer. The women did agree to meet once again before Lou and Amelia returned to Connecticut. They hugged warmly, then with Adelaide's diary and Dr. Sam's telephone number in hand, Lou and Amelia left Galynn Hall to begin the short drive back to their hotel room.

CHAPTER 15

Winfield Farm

Amelia calculated that Dr. Cotter must be, at the very least, in his early eighties. "I certainly hope Dr. Cotter is well enough to help us, Granny Lou."

"Well, let's find out right now!" With determination, Lou began to dial up Dr. Cotter's number. "Worse- case scenario, there may be any number of reasons why he or his children may not be able or willing to help us. Though, should that be the case, all would not be lost. Actually, Beth has already provided us with the answer to our question concerning the family origin of your name. We know that Adelaide named her adopted daughter, Amelia. Amelia Currick Gale had not been named for anyone within her adoptive or biological family. Only her middle name, Currick, comes from her biological family. That means there are no other descendents with the given name, Amelia. We could simply stop here."

Amelia felt her heart sink deep within her chest. "Granny Lou, what are you saying? Don't you want to know what could have happened to her? Surely, she would not have intentionally inflicted so much pain upon her loving mother and family!"

Lou's expression of surprise, mirrored Amelia's own reaction to her resurrected passion. "My you look wonderfully aghast; I have not seen so much expression on your face, in sometime. Now, don't fret, we are not going to end our efforts here. I just don't want you to be disappointed if we…" Lou abruptly stopped talking, and placed a finger to her lips before speaking into the phone.

"Hello, my name is Lou McDowell, and I would like to speak with Dr. Samuel Cotter." Lou crossed her fingers in front of her face.

"This is, Melissa Cotter, my father is not available at the moment. May I take a message and ask him to return your call?"

"Yes, please." Lou repeated her name and gave the hotel phone number. "I was referred to Dr. Cotter, by Beth Bissett. My granddaughter and I have just spent the day with Beth discussing family genealogy. Beth felt that possibly, Dr. Cotter might be able to provide us with additional information."

There was a long pause before Melissa answered. "Well, I will ask my father to return your call when he returns from grand rounds."

In an obvious fluster, Lou responded. "Oh, I am looking for the senior Dr. Samuel Cotter."

Melissa laughed. "There's only one Dr. Samuel Cotter! As long as RUMC invites him to attend grand rounds, and the good Lord so wills it, he will hobble over there on his eighty-five years old legs, and share his sixty-four years of medical experience."

Lou's mouth curled into an amused smile. "Well, thank you very much Ms. Cotter; I look forward to speaking with your father."

"Well, what did she say?" Amelia no longer tried to camouflage her emotional involvement.

"As you heard, Dr. Cotter was not in. I spoke with his daughter. She will have him call me back when he returns; so we just wait." Lou patted her stomach. "I don't know about you Amelia, but that delicious breakfast Beth had prepared for us is wearing off. How about we order up an early dinner, and eat in our room? That way we will not miss Dr. Cotter's call."

"Sounds good; anything, for the cause! Besides, that will give me an opportunity to read through Adelaide's diary." Amelia moved herself to the round table in the corner of the room, where she had placed the diary. In the meantime, Lou ordered up their food before lying down for a short nap.

Dinner arrived at 6:00 PM. Over a course of grilled sword fish and fries, Amelia reviewed for her grandmother the latest secrets she had uncovered from Adelaide's diary. "There is no doubt that Adelaide was a detail person; not too much escaped her notice. For instance, she describes in great detail everyone's reaction to Amelia, when as an infant, she was brought to Galynn Hall. Adelaide's documented observation of events continues well into her daughter's formative years."

Amelia did not stop to eat but continued. "It's funny, probably because our names are the same, I sometimes feel like I am talking about myself. But anyway, apparently at first there was some sibling rivalry between Everton and his new sister. It seems Everton had suffered an injury to his right arm, during his birth. As he grew, the injury continued to cause considerable atrophy and deformity of the arm."

Lou looked thoughtful. "The defect must have been camouflaged in the family portrait."

Amelia shook her head in agreement. "I'm sure it had been. There is more. Though blameless and coming close to losing her own life, Adelaide was guilt ridden. Consequently, she doted upon her youngest son. With a new sister in the picture, it was no longer possible for Adelaide to shower unlimited time and attention upon the youngster."

"In response to his mother's preoccupation with the baby, Everton would often respond with terrible tantrums. Despite this troubling beginning, Amelia over time would win her brother's affection. It seemed that with sibling rivalry behind him, eventually Everton came to adore his sister."

Lou, between bites of her food managed to question Amelia. "What was the relationship between Mazzie Winfield and the child?"

"Well, remember that Mazzie was a year older than Everton when the baby was brought to Galynn Hall. Though never physically abused, she had been born into slavery, and certainly by the age of five, would have known her place. Possibly, that is why there had never been any jealousy between the girls. In fact, from all accounts, Mazzie behaved instinctively motherly toward the infant. Through the years, Adelaide would often trust her over other house servants to watch her daughter for short periods of time. As the girls grow, the bond between them did as well; throughout their childhood they had watched over one another."

"Several pages into the diary, Adelaide writes about her dismay over the closeness which had developed between the girls. As kind as she had always been, she worried about how it appeared for her daughter to prefer the friendship of a slave over other girls her age."

"Over the years, Everton had become progressively more possessive of his younger sister, and resented her affection for Mazzie. At one point he had threatened to beat Mazzie within an inch of her life if she did not learn her place and stop behaving like Amelia's sister. Fortunately, Mazzie's fate rested with Adelaide. In the end, Amelia's loving ways always melted her mother's heart, so that even her untenable relationship with Mazzie had been sanctioned by all, save Everton."

Amelia ended her critique with the realization that the story had become more to her than just an exercise her grandmother had devised in order to help her to overcome her melancholy. The more she learned about Amelia Currick Gale the more she yearned to know every detail of her life.

Following Amelia's thorough review of the diary, Lou

asserted her maternal authority. "Oh, my dear, forgive me for asking you so many questions. From start to finish, you had me mesmerized. But in the meantime your dinner sits untouched beneath that metal cover. Now, please eat your food. Your mother will personally excommunicate me from the family should I bring you home one pound lighter."

Not long after Lou and Amelia finished their food, the phone rang. Lou winked at Amelia and lifted the receiver. "Hello, Lou McDowell speaking."

The baritone voice on the other end of the line was strong with a slight southern twang. "Hello, Ms. McDowell, this is Dr. Samuel Cotter returning your call. I understand that you are acquainted with Beth Bissett, and that you were hoping I could help you with a family genealogy question. Is that correct?"

After thanking Dr. Cotter for returning her call, Lou clarified for the good doctor, her reason for contacting him.

"So, you are telling me that you are a descendent of Amelia Currick Gale, and are trying to unravel the 150 year old mystery surrounding her disappearance. Do I have that right?" Once again, Dr. Cotter waited for Lou's confirmation.

With usual candor, Lou replied. "That pretty much sums it up."

"Well, if Beth has already spoken with you and believes I might be of assistance, please by all means let us meet. I have no appointments tomorrow. Doctor's orders, you see, I am forced to rest up at least three days out of the week. Would it be convenient for you to stop by the farm tomorrow, about 10:00 AM?"

Lou thanked Dr. Cotter for his invitation and willingly agreed to meet with him the following day.

*   *   *   *

Amelia reveled in the suspense; she wondered where the Amelia Currick Gale mystery might take them next. During the short drive to Winfield Farm, she seized the opportunity to quiz Lou on her strategy. "Granny Lou, what exactly are you hoping Dr. Cotter will tell us?"

Lou reviewed the information they had already gathered, as well as the missing pieces needed before they could leave the area with the mystery solved. "Amelia, it always comes back to the question as to why Amelia Currick Gale had left her loving family. Next, of importance is an understanding as to whether or not Mazzie Winfield played any part in the disappearance. Lastly, did our ancestral grandmother's disappearance have anything to do with the rather unorthodox land transaction? We can only hope that Dr. Cotter is willing and able to answer those three questions."

Lou turned a sharp right into the long drive leading to Winfield Farm. Amelia spotted a number of structures dotting the pastoral landscape. She thought it charming that all the buildings remained consistent with the original nineteenth century architecture. Somehow, the farm had managed to retain its historical functionality as well as its Southern charm. She noted two large barns on the property, seemingly designated to house the larger animals. The ground surrounding a smaller barn lay carpeted in feathers, and the clucking sound coming from within its walls, clearly indicated that this was the chicken coop.

A modest two-story home, meticulously maintained, stood at the end of a two mile long driveway. The home's aura was neither melancholy nor foreboding, yet Amelia sensed the indelible hold of past centuries. The expansive, wraparound porch seemed to reach out to the visitors in welcome. In the front yard, two small black children stopped their play to wave. Lou and Amelia smiled and waved back to them, before making their way up the three wooden steps leading to the porch.

Lou rang the door bell and a statuesque black woman with angular features made her appearance. "Please, come on in Mrs. McDowell, I'm Melissa Cotter. And this must be your granddaughter, come on in, dear."

Amelia said a polite hello, while Lou took Melissa's hand in greeting. "Yes, this is my granddaughter, Amelia Morelli."

"It is nice to meet you. My father will be down shortly, he is cleaning himself up after spending the earlier part of the morning trying to talk them chickens into laying more eggs." Melissa shook her head and added. "He never slows down; it's impossible to get Dr. Sam to follow the doctor's orders!"

Lou replied. "I understand and I promise you, we will not overtax your father. We so very much appreciate his willingness to speak with us."

"Well, if anyone can help you it is my father, he was very close with his grandmother. Fortunately, she lived well into her nineties and he had many years with her. In fact, Papa is probably the only person alive who might have information to share with you concerning the relationship between the Winfield family and the Gales. His two older siblings had left the area in their early twenties and have since passed on." Melissa looked suddenly embarrassed. "Oh forgive me, I am forgetting my manners; can I get you tea or coffee?"

"No, thank you, Amelia and I just finished a filling breakfast."

"Well then, please excuse me; I will see what is keeping that man." Melissa hastily left her guests.

Within minutes of Melissa's departure the parlor door opened and an elderly gentleman entered the room. Unlike his daughter, Dr. Cotter was a short, slight man, with a light complexion and discerning brown eyes. The frail man warmly shook hands with Lou and Amelia, and welcomed them to Winfield Farm. At the sound of Dr. Cotter's deep baritone voice, Amelia noted a look of recognition upon her grandmother's face. "So what can I tell you about my paternal grandmother, other than, I have been blessed to have had her in my life. You know she was 77 years old at my birth in

1917; we were given twenty two years together. Even on her deathbed, her humor remained intact; she joked that in order to keep me out of trouble she had stayed in this God forsaken place as long as she had. Mind you, despite her sarcasm, she was very much the optimist."

Lou interjected. "It sounds as though you and your grandmother were very close!"

"Yes, we were. She was a wonderful woman, as was your distant grandmother, Amelia Currick Gale. At the risk of sounding impertinent, had you and your charming granddaughter not been blood relations to the lady in question, it is most unlikely we would be having this conversation."

Dr. Cotter quickly continued. "My grandmother confided in me many heartwarming details of the relationship she had shared with Miss Amelia. Had it not been for Miss Amelia, my grandmother would have most likely remained illiterate. You do know that during slavery it was prohibited to teach a Negro to read and write? As my grandmother expressed it, Miss Amelia put up a demure fuss in order for the young black slave to be schooled with her." Dr. Cotter shook his head. "*Out of the mouth of babes*! But, before I rattle on, what precisely are you trying to uncover?"

Amelia could no longer restrain herself. Taking a deep breath, she spoke out before Lou could utter a word. "Dr. Cotter, we have been researching the life of our ancestor for many months. My grandmother and I feel as though we knew both Miss Amelia and Mazzie. We do not believe they were just two selfish girls, who simply ran away, though heaven only knows, Mazzie certainly had cause. Contrary to the news paper articles of the day, we could find no reason to believe that Mazzie would have ever harmed Miss Amelia." To her surprise, Amelia felt her eyes moisten with tears. "Please, help us; we just do not want to leave not knowing the truth behind their disappearance."

Dr. Cotter looked long at the lovely young girl. "Amelia,

pardon me, if I ask you the obvious, but were you by chance named for Amelia Currick Gale?"

Amelia without hesitation, answered yes.

"You have much to be proud of, and even more to live up to. I can tell you this, Miss Amelia and my grandmother did leave that fateful night on November 28, 1860. With the help of Quaker families and abolitionists working within the Underground Railroad, the two young women made their way to New York City. While living in the North, Mazzie was able to secure work as a seamstress. Sometime later, Miss Amelia resurfaced and began working as a language tutor for the children of a prominent New York family. Even if the family had suspected who Miss Amelia was, they had strong ties to abolitionist factions in both the North and South. It goes without saying they would have had little sympathy for slaveholders and would not have turned the girls over to authorities. Also, soon after the ladies impromptu departure from Virginia, the state had seceded from the Union and the war was on."

Dr. Cotter continued without interruption. "By all accounts, the war was hell, though what followed was equally painful. Contrary to the misconception of many folks living in the North, the Reconstruction Period proved devastating for both the white and black man living in the South. Black men and women were freed with no place to go. They were ill equipped to make a living either in the South or the North. While most of the plantation owners in the area were fortunate enough to have retained their land holdings, everything else including their livestock, equipment and slave labor, had been taken from them. Many an unscrupulous plantation owner would hire former slaves back for a pittance, only to deny the sorry lot their earnings once the job was completed. Richmond was in ruins, with its people, white and black, dying in the streets of starvation. God in his infinite mercy had at least spared Miss Amelia the horror of Reconstruction."

"So, Mazzie did return in 1872, to face the Reconstruction period?" Lou pushed for clarification.

Dr. Cotter reflected. "Yes, I believe she had said 1872. She returned only to endure the Black Codes, the Jim Crow laws, and the Ku Klux Klan, along with the rest of us. Miss Amelia never returned to Virginia. Instead she met and married a Presbyterian minister, whom she had been introduced to while staying at the Stamford, Connecticut, summer home of her employer. She proceeded to have two children, and worked beside her husband until the end of her days in 1918. She died a year after my birth. I believe you must be privy to the rest of her history."

Lou probed further. "Yes, you are correct; we have a good account of Miss Amelia's life in Connecticut. But, why did Mazzie return?"

"Mazzie had her ways of keeping abreast of what had become of those she had left behind. She knew that her mother, Pearl, had been ailing for some time. She was also aware that Pearl had secured Winfield Farm."

Before Dr. Cotter could continue, Lou once again posed a question. "But surely Dr. Cotter, Pearl would not have had the means to buy land. Nor was her right to buy land sanctioned by the law at that time. How did such a transaction come about?"

It seemed to Amelia, that Dr. Cotter had anticipated Lou's question and was ready with his answer. Calmly he posed his explanation. "You see, well before his father's death in 1870, Justin Gale had virtually taken over the operation of Galynn Hall, as well as the family's other land holdings. According to my grandmother, Justin was Adelaide's son in every sense of the word. The humanity he had extended to the helpless and downtrodden under his charge in years past was rewarded during those dark days. Both blacks and whites were far more inclined to work for a man they felt would not cheat them or do far worse by them. He was known for his generosity, and in more than one instance, had given up land to sharecroppers and house slaves who had worked for him over the years."

The incredulous look upon her grandmother's face, did not escape Amelia's notice. She knew Dr. Cotter had seen her grandmother's expression as well. Now with determination in her voice, Lou probed further. "Is that the only reason you believe Justin Gale had awarded Pearl Winfield, 342 acres of the Gale family land and had continued to protect the Winfield holdings?"

Dr. Cotter lowered his head and quickly concluded. "That is all I can tell you!"

"Please, Dr. Cotter do you have any idea as to why the two women had left in the first place?" Lou's tone had become imploring.

Dr. Cotter spoke slowly and the muscles around his eyes and mouth sagged beneath his smooth brown skin. "I can only deduct that the young women had some sort of a pact which would lead to Mazzie's liberation."

Amelia felt for the elderly man, realizing that the dialogue was taking its toll upon him. She knew what a formidable interrogator her Granny Lou could be. Fortunately, for Dr. Cotter, Lou was also a very kind person. Amelia was not in the least surprised when her grandmother abruptly ended the interview.

"Dr. Cotter, I believe it is time for us to take our leave. I thank you from the bottom of my heart for all you have shared with us, as well as for your warm hospitality. Please take my address and telephone number. I would be grateful if you would contact me should you recall any additional information pertinent to our quest." Lou warmly shook Dr. Cotter's hand, while Amelia said a soulful goodbye, before leaving the old gentleman at the door.

Discouraged, though not disheartened, Lou and Amelia began their drive back to the hotel. Amelia's curiosity once again got the best of her, and before the car had left Winfield

Farm, she confronted her grandmother. "So, Granny Lou, what do you think?"

"I believe Dr. Cotter to be a very intelligent gentleman. Regardless of his young age when he interacted with Mazzie, I doubt he would have left his grandmother off the hook quite so easily." Lou arched her left brow as she often did when mentally dissecting a puzzling piece of information.

"What do you mean by that?"

Lou took a deep breath. "I mean that Dr. Cotter knows more than what he shared with us today. I do not believe for one moment that Amelia Currick Gale would have left her mother never to return in order to secure Mazzie's freedom. I believe she would have assisted Mazzie, while remaining at Galynn Hall. Also, it is just plain ridiculous to imagine that even the kind Justin Gale would have deposited 342 acres into the lap of one of his former slaves for no other reason than his generosity fueled by guilt."

"So, what can we do now?" Amelia asked.

"Nothing, we may have to be satisfied with what we have learned thus far. If the good Lord wants us to know more, we will! Tomorrow morning we shall return the diary to Beth Bissett and begin our drive back to Connecticut."

Amelia recognized the look of satisfied finality upon Lou's face. Even though many questions surrounding the historic mystery remained unanswered, she knew her grandmother was at peace with what they had learned. Amelia only hoped for that same sense of closure in respect to the Amelia Currick Gale mystery, as well as other issues complicating her young life.

CHAPTER 16

Lessons from The Past

Lou stared into the computer screen, her eyes focusing upon the last sentence of her manuscript. She found it hard to believe that three and a half months had passed since she and Amelia had returned from their trip to Charles City, Virginia. Within that time, she had completed the final draft of her book. And she was satisfied to be able to incorporate much of what she and Amelia had learned about basic genealogy. She only wished that her expectations for Amelia's improvement were as easy to determine. Though very proud of the girl for managing to complete her junior year in High School with a 4.0 average, Lou and the rest of the family continued to fret amongst themselves about her apparent lack of direction.

Karen regularly reported that Amelia had not touched her Baby Grand piano, and remained taciturn concerning any career plans. With no one yet able to bridge the crevice of silence, Amelia's problems remained as much a mystery as had her ancestral grandmother's disappearance from Virginia. After considerable trial and error, Lou concluded it best to abide by her own advice and refrain from broaching the forbidden issues with her granddaughter. It had become painfully clear to everyone, that fruitful discussion would take place on Amelia's terms, alone.

Lou took a deep breath, at the very least she was grateful for the subtle changes she had observed in her granddaughter's demeanor. Also, there was her book, finally ready to be emailed to her publicist.

Following hours in front of her computer, Lou stopped for her well earned coffee break. She placed the ground Brazilian coffee beans into the coffee maker, before venturing to the front door to retrieve the daily newspaper and morning mail.

Usually Lou missed the mailman by at least a good hour. Today was different, when she opened the front door she found herself face to face with Jake. Lou knew by his expression that he was as startled, as was she.

"Good morning, Mrs. McDowell! I was just about to ring your door bell. I have a certified letter for you; if you would please sign right here behind the X."

Lou regained her composure, signing as directed in her definitive bold script. "Jake, you must be running late; I don't usually bump into you. Thank you for the letter; I wonder what this could be? Well, anyway, have a good day!"

"You do the same, Mrs. McDowell!" Without explanation, Jake hurried away.

Once inside the house, Lou inspected the small brown envelope. The return address read Winfield Farm, followed by Melissa Cotter's name, rather than her father's. When Lou opened the brown envelope she found a short handwritten note from Melissa. In the note, Melissa stated that her beloved father had passed away two weeks earlier. She went on to explain that soon after Lou's visit, her father had drafted a letter and placed it into a sealed envelope. He requested that the envelope be mailed to Lou immediately following his death. He was emphatic that the letter was for Lou's eyes only; stating that he would not have given his daughter the letter had he not been certain she would do as he had requested.

Lou was both surprised to receive the correspondence, as well as saddened to learn of Dr. Cotter's passing. With care, she opened the enclosed envelope and began reading the lengthy correspondence. Lou guessed, that Dr. Cotter had meticulously typed the letter on heavy, durable paper so that she would not experience difficulty deciphering a handwritten letter. As Lou read she hung on to every word, while at the same time envisioning the old man's sympathetic face. When she finished reading, she wiped the tears from her soft hazel eyes. She was more than grateful for the trust he had placed in her. Vigorously, she blew her nose as though in protest of her bout with sentimentality.

Lou's pragmatism quickly took rein over her sentiments. When and where would she present the letter to Amelia? She thought long and hard on the matter. Eventually, she decided on what she believed to be the ideal place to share Dr. Cotter's letter with her granddaughter.

*　　*　　*　　*

It was the end of July. Amelia dressed in cut off jeans and a yellow halter-top, waited for her grandmother's car to pull into the drive. Though the day promised to be picture perfect with low humidity and cooling, offshore winds, her mind was not on the weather. Rather, she was more than curious as to why Granny Lou wanted to return to the Stamford family gravesite. The same gravesite they had discovered several months earlier.

At 10:30 AM sharp, Granny Lou's car pulled into the driveway. With the expected exuberance of a sixteen year old, Amelia hopped into her grandmother's SUV. "See, Granny Lou, I'm on time once again. Now, why are we returning to the Covenant Presbyterian Chapel cemetery? Did we miss something when we first visited there?"

"Oh, no dear; actually I have a surprise for you! I thought I might share the surprise with you at the cemetery, and then we could have our lunch under the trees. Remember our excitement the day we first discovered the forgotten gravesites of Amelia Currick Gale, Edan Thomas and their son Currick. To think so much of our family history had played out just fifty miles from New Haven."

Amelia frowned. "I guess I'll have to wait for the surprise? Anyway, I'll never understand why the congregation left such an idyllic site. It reminded me of those beautiful pastoral scenes painted by *Currier and Ives.*"

"Well, Amelia, yes to your first question. Now, remember we had talked about how the small chapel had apparently been abandoned to build a larger church closer to the hub of Stamford."

Within an hour Lou and Amelia reached their destination. Rather than walking directly to the graveyard, they made their way to the old chapel. Lou pressed on the latch of the heavy wooden door. She looked surprised when the latch clicked and the creaking door slowly opened.

Amelia shrugged her shoulders. "I wonder why the door was locked the first time we were here. Do you think we should be entering this old building; don't you feel like a trespasser?"

"Well, not exactly, but you may have a point about entering the building. We certainly do not know if it is structurally sound." As Lou peered into the chapel, she stopped talking and just stared. Her eyes remained fixated upon a magnificent stained glass window high above the altar. "Oh Amelia, you must see this. Look at the light beaming through that window. How do you suppose that work of art had survived so many decades of neglect?"

Cautiously, Amelia positioned herself in front of her grandmother, poking her head farther into the doorway. From this vantage point she was able to view the window. The window depicted the image of a large Celtic cross supported by the saints of old. The top of the cross was surrounded by a crown of several fair haired angels. At first glance, Amelia was convinced that the angels mirrored the likeness of her ancestral grandmother. "I don't know Granny Lou, either God's angels had a hand in preserving that work of art or the workman whose tools are scattered about had something to do with it." Prompted by a rush of confidence, Amelia motioned her grandmother into the chapel.

Amelia led the way, while Lou tiptoed into the building. "Well, you are right. It looks like someone is in the process of restoring this old chapel. Though, I would like to think it was God who preserved that window. When we first discovered this place, I was stymied as to why the chapel had not been restored years ago. Both the chapel and its cemetery are historical treasures."

Lou and Amelia looked up once again; for a second they stood mesmerized by the pastel colored rainbow radiating through the circular window. Lou spoke as though, to herself. "Strange, that with all those large oak trees looming over the sanctuary, that any light would find its way to illuminate that breathtaking, masterpiece. You might very well imagine that the entire scene had been orchestrated by none other than Amelia Currick Gale."

Spurred on by Lou's words, they cautiously made their way farther into the chapel. Close to the front of the sanctuary, they seated themselves upon one of the restored pews. Paradoxically, Amelia found the quietness of the setting to be electrifying. "Granny Lou, it feels like Ms. Amelia and Edan are here with us, and I can almost envision what it must have been like so long ago. Is this the surprise you wanted to share with me?"

"No, dear, this is a surprise for me as well! My scripted surprise is actually a letter I had received from Dr. Cotter, last week. I was planning to read it to you while we picnicked along the cemetery wood line. As fate would have it, this is probably a far more appropriate setting." Lou removed her reading glasses and Dr. Cotter's letter from her shoulder bag. Placing the glasses upon her face, she began with a short account of events. "Actually, Melissa Cotter mailed the letter. Unfortunately, Dr. Cotter had passed on three weeks earlier. I will read the letter to you so we can both share his words together." Lou took a deep breath in preparation for reading the lengthy letter.

Once again that familiar ache, deep within her solar plexus, caught Amelia off guard. With a sorrowful frown, she interrupted her grandmother. "Granny Lou, Dr. Cotter seemed so kind; in many ways he reminded me of Uncle Stew! Why do such good people have to leave us?"

Lou pulled her granddaughter close to her. "I don't have all the answers for you darling; but maybe this letter will help us both to better understand the sanity of events." With deliberation, Lou began to read.

April 30, 2003

My Dearest Mrs. McDowell,

If you are reading this letter you are well aware that I have since joined my dearly departed loved ones, including my precious grandmother, Mazzie. Know that the burdens of this world no longer weigh heavy upon me. Had it not been for our chance meeting, my resolve had been to take the history I am about to share with you, to my grave. I believe little if any purpose would be served in burdening anyone else with this information, especially my own children. If I had been less persistent and precocious as a seventeen-year old lad, my grandmother would have died with this information, as I believe, Amelia Currick Gale had. Following her clear communication of the facts, Mazzie had me promise not to share what she had told me, with anyone. I believe she would not find fault with me for what I plan to do under these new and unexpected circumstances. I also trust that you and your granddaughter will do right by all concerned.

No more than two weeks following your visit on this April 11th, I met Beth Bissett. We both serve on the Richmond Community Service Committee. Though she was well apprised of our meeting, I believe she was more than curious as to whether I had revealed new information to you, which she had not been privy to. I think you would agree that Beth is quite the consummate historian! During our conversation, she mentioned that your granddaughter had recently lost her father in the September 11th tragedy. There was something about your granddaughter; when she first implored me to share what I knew about her ancestral grandmother, she pulled at my heartstrings. After learning this additional information, I was struck by the parallels between her young life, and the life of Amelia Currick Gale. Both women had suffered profound loss at a very early age. This world spares no one, we can only pray that when we touch another's life, that our words and actions only help to alleviate the pain our brothers and sisters may be experiencing. I hope you and your granddaughter will take comfort in the knowledge that both Amelia Currick Gale and my grandmother, Mazzie, worked for good in the lives of those they had touched. Both were exceptional women. So my good lady, this is why I share the following with you. This is meant exclusively for you and your lovely granddaughter. I trust that the information in this letter will not be shared with anyone else.

It all began with the Williamsburg Cotillion, the month and year of September 1860. All but two and a half months later, the girls would leave Virginia. Malin Gale had intended to present his daughter at the gala event. This event would give Ms. Amelia the opportunity to meet and mingle with the most accomplished and wealthy young men in the region. As fate would have it, Malin and Justin had been delayed due to problems in Roanoke involving a hired overseer and plantation slaves. Adelaide had been ill, and regardless, her gender prohibited her from introducing her daughter at the Cotillion. The only suitable member of the family available to escort Miss Amelia had been Everton. Adelaide had been most unhappy about this turn of events. She knew full well, that Everton was known to drown his frustrations with drink. She attributed this short coming to the young man's inability to come to terms with his deformed right arm. The arm had been damaged during his birth. As Everton grew into manhood he had become increasingly resentful of both his brother, Justin, and Miss Amelia's maid servant, Mazzie. While he resented Justin for being whole of body and mind, he was jealous of the time Amelia spent with Mazzie, as well as the affection they shared. Though, Miss Amelia was the one family member able to subdue Everton when his behavior became troublesome, Adelaide felt uneasy about the arrangement. Her only recourse was to suggest that Mazzie accompany her daughter, as well. Of course, Everton would not hear of it, so he alone escorted the sixteen-year old girl.

My grandmother remembered that Miss Amelia had looked like an angel. The lilac taffeta gown she wore that night was long and flowing. Her golden hair swept up, created a halo affect atop of those dancing green eyes. Happy to be stepping out as Richmond's most desirable debutante, the young damsel sparkled. As might be expected, Miss Amelia had many admirers that night, dancing with several prospective suitors. Only after the ball had ended, did things start to turn badly for the young woman. It seems that while Miss Amelia had danced the night away, Everton had proceeded to drown his jealousy over her flirtations, with an indulgence of spirits.

As arranged days earlier, Miss Amelia and Everton were to stay the night with distant cousins living in Williamsburg. The home was within walking distance of where the cotillion had been held. Miss Amelia, realizing the extent to which Everton was intoxicated, suggested they spend some time walking in a nearby park, so to expedite her brother's return to sobriety. During the walk Everton became belligerent, accusing Miss Amelia of flaunting her charms in front of drooling swine. Miss Amelia was mortified, to say the least, but nothing she said would quiet

Everton's fury. The young man continued to rant, stating that he alone was suitable to take Miss Amelia's hand in marriage. Amelia stunned, questioned why any man would want to marry his sister. The piercing words that followed had remained with Miss Amelia until her dying day. Everton shouted. "You are no more my sister than your nigger, Mazzie, is! Amelia, haven't you figured it out yet? Currick, you were adopted!"

The blood drained from Miss Amelia's face, though she still had the strength to challenge Everton. "That's not true, why are you saying such an awful thing?"

Everton's response went something like this. "As a teenager, many a late night, I would eavesdrop at our parent's bedroom door. More often, than not, they were discussing how best to deal with their prodigal son. On one of those nights, I believe I was fifteen, I overheard mother and father discussing when best to reveal to you your true parentage. Mother said that she felt it best to wait until you were suitably married. She had been afraid that if people knew the truth, you might experience the same ostracism she had, upon arriving from the Netherlands, as father's bride."

Miss Amelia refused to believe her brother, stating that he was drunk and had made the entire lie up. Things grew progressively heated, until Everton would control his lust for Miss Amelia not a moment longer. Hidden within the shadows of the park, he pulled the trembling girl to him. He ardently professed his love, and stated that her parentage made little if any difference to him. Then the unthinkable took place, and Everton sexually forced himself upon Miss Amelia. Physically, Miss Amelia was no match for the strong young man. Any effort on her part to fight off Everton's advances, made him more determined to have his way with her. After Everton had had his way, Miss Amelia pleaded to be taken back to Galynn Hall.

During the weeks that followed, she suffered quietly. She feared rejection or worse, the destruction of her family should the truth about that awful evening be made known. The last person she wanted to hurt or bring shame upon was Adelaide.

Unfortunately, things had gone from very bad to intolerable when Miss Amelia began to suspect that she was pregnant with Everton's child.

Adelaide, as well as the rest of the family, had noticed a dramatic change in the girl's demeanor. Once a happy and lively teenager, Miss Amelia had become reclusive and listless. Physically, the girl had lost weight, and her eyes once expressive and alive, were now dull and lost. Adelaide was at her wit's end; she could not fathom what might be causing her daughter's melancholy. Believing Miss Amelia to be physically ill, the distraught woman insisted that she be seen by the family physician. Frantic that her secret would soon be revealed, Miss Amelia poured out her heart to her trusted maid servant, Mazzie.

My grandmother remembered that she had never come closer to murdering another human being, then the day that Miss Amelia had confided in her the truth of her circumstances. Without hesitation, she advised Miss Amelia to go to Adelaide with the truth. My grandmother knew full well, the love Adelaide and the rest of the family had for the girl. All involved, were acutely aware of Everton's problems; she was certain that in this instance bloodlines would not take precedence. Unfortunately, Miss Amelia flatly refused to do such a thing. She insisted that her only recourse was to leave for the North, traveling as far from Richmond as possible.

Mazzie refused to let Miss Amelia leave without her. Both young women realized the risks for Mazzie, whether she stayed behind, or left with her mistress. Though never insistent that Mazzie accompany her, Miss Amelia expressed her profound relief when the slave whom she loved as a sister, stood firm in her refusal to let her go alone.

So they made the arduous journey together, finally arriving in New York City in mid March of 1861. With a small amount of money Miss Amelia had taken with her, the two women rented a rundown flat in the heart of the big city. Time had proven Miss Amelia's fear to be true; upon reaching their destination, she was six months into her pregnancy. Without adequate nourishment or the basic comforts, both women had suffered ill effects. Due to her pregnancy, Miss Amelia's health had been compromised more so than Mazzie's had. Even under the best of circumstances, Miss Amelia had always been the physically frailer of the two women. Mazzie did what she could to keep her mistress healthy, sometimes giving the young woman her own rations. Despite Mazzie's efforts, Miss Amelia at the end of their destination was both physically and emotionally spent. Less than a month later, on April 17, 1861, Mazzie assisted her mistress in the birth of a stillborn baby boy. Ironically, the birth occurred on the very day that Virginia had seceded from the Union.

Further weakened by the delivery and later hemorrhaging, Miss Amelia spent most of the following year in a fight for her own survival. Mazzie refused to let Miss Amelia die, tending to the young woman when not working as a seamstress.

Through newspaper articles, as well as the hearsay of runaway slaves from Richmond, Mazzie would learn the fate of loved ones from home who had been caught up in the war. During the summer of 1863, while in conversation with a runaway slave, turned Union soldier, Mazzie learned of Adelaide's passing during that same spring. Her heart sank, as she had loved Adelaide. To make matters worse, she could not bear the thought, that at some point, she would have to tell Miss Amelia the fate of her mother. Her only consolation rested in the knowledge that Richmond to date had escaped many horrors of the war. As the Capitol of the Confederacy, Richmond and its outlying areas had been far better protected against Union insurgence. In all probability, Adelaide had escaped those same horrors that Mazzie feared would eventually come to Richmond's door.

In time, Miss Amelia's health had improved. Eventually she had secured employment as a foreign language tutor for the children of a wealthy New York family. I do believe that I had mentioned this during your visit. It was sometime in the fall of 1863, when Mazzie mustered up enough courage to share the news of Adelaide's fate with Miss Amelia. Of course, Miss Amelia was beside herself with guilt. There had been little Mazzie could do or say to alleviate the young woman's pain. Had Mazzie not been brought up in slavery, and seen her people survive unfathomable hardship, she would not have believed that Miss Amelia could survive yet another mortal blow in her young life.

As unbelievable as it might seem, together both women did survive. The bloody war finally came to an end, though for many years to come the misery continued in the South. Eventually, Miss Amelia adapted to Northern life; marrying a Presbyterian minister at age 23 years. From that union she would give birth to two healthy boys. Miss Amelia had begged my grandmother to move out of the New York flat and join her in Connecticut, but Mazzie had other plans. She had never adapted to city life or the colder northern climate. Also, she never stopped missing Pearl's wise counsel. Her dream remained, to return to Virginia as a free woman. Satisfied that Miss Amelia had been able to continue with her life, Mazzie in spite of the risks had every intention of returning to her home. As fate would have it, one evening in April 1871, there was a knock on Mazzie's door. To her astonishment, Justin Gale stood in the doorway. Always the gentleman, Justin never accused Mazzie of any conceivable wrong. Rather, he pleaded with her to share what information she might have concerning his long missing sister.

Mazzie in turn, questioned Justin as to how he had come to find her after ten long years. He explained that one of his runaway field slaves who had lived in New York, had learned of Mazzie's whereabouts. Following the end of the war, this same Negro worked his way back to Richmond. Remembering that there had been a reward offered for information pertaining to Mazzie and Miss Amelia's disappearance, he approached Justin Gale. Two months following Malin Gale's death, Justin decided he would make the trip north to check on the validity of the black man's story.

At first dazed by Justin's appearance at her door, Mazzie

quickly regained her composure. She wasted little time agonizing over what she would share with Justin, concerning the events of the past ten years. She knew that the truth must finally be made known; and she adamantly believed that the truth needed to come from Miss Amelia's lips. A face to face meeting between brother and sister would have to take place.

That same evening, Mazzie made necessary arrangements with her employer and prepared for a trip to Stamford, Connecticut. Justin was able to secure lodging for the night. In anticipation of their journey, neither Mazzie nor Justin slept well that night. Even so, the following morning they were up early and ready to begin their journey to Miss Amelia's home.

My grandmother could only imagine the extent of Miss Amelia's ambivalence when she and Justin walked through her door. They entered the small house to find Ms. Amelia alone with her sleeping young sons, while her husband worked at his church. The grown woman flew into Justin's open arms, just as she had as a child growing up at Galynn Hall. Tears of joy and anticipation flowed down their faces. Mazzie just watched holding back her own tears. Justin was the first to speak. "Thank God you are alive, we all feared you were dead. Amelia, please tell me what happened? Why would you leave a mother who had loved you more than herself? My dear, dear, sister, please tell me!"

Momentarily, Miss Amelia spoke. "You, call me sister, did you not know I had been adopted as an infant?"

Justin looked dumbfounded; this was hardly what he had expected to hear. He responded with thoughtful words. "Following your disappearance, and still later after our mother's death, there had never been a word to me concerning this matter. Even if that is the truth, you shall always be my sister. Certainly as a ten year old boy, I was surprised when Mother and Father returned from Roanoke with a baby. Mother simply explained that due to her difficult pregnancies she did not want to worry Everton or me, with news that she was again pregnant. Consequently, she explained that she had accompanied Father to Roanoke where she had always claimed she give birth to you. Any doubts, anyone may have had concerning circumstances of your birth, were soon to be forgotten. You see, you were so like Mother, in every aspect of her being. Why would you think such a thing?"

With unbridled emotion, Miss Amelia answered. "Because I had been adopted at birth, and I learned of this two and a half months before I left Galynn Hall."

"Is that why you left us?" Justin pleaded.

Miss Amelia hesitated, realizing that her interrogation might end here. Before the distraught woman could answer, Mazzie spoke the words she had held back for many years. "Miss Amelia, please for all of our sakes, you must tell Justin the truth, he must know!"

Apparently, Miss Amelia's heart had told her that Mazzie spoke wisely. She began her difficult explanation. When she had finished, Justin took his sister in his arms as if she were a child. He repeated his heart-felt apology several times over. Following what had seemed an eternity of silence, Justin again spoke. "My brother no longer can be taken to task for his heinous act. You see he was killed in combat during the war. Amelia, what if anything, can I do to make amends for Everton's unimaginable actions?"

Adoringly, Miss Amelia looked up at the large man, once again remembering the comfort he had always provided her as a small child. Speaking softly, she answered. "Just being here, you have done so much already!"

Justin's face brightened. "Your inheritance, Amelia, just think of what that could mean to your young family. Half of our father's estate is rightfully yours."

Miss Amelia looked surprised. "Has father passed on as well?"

Justin hung his head. "Yes, he died over two months ago. You were always in his thoughts, and then when he lost Mother, he was never the same man. Please Amelia, let me try and make this right by you; you have lost so much."

Miss Amelia lifted her lovely face, looking more at peace

than Mazzie had seen her in years. At that moment, Miss Amelia spoke the words that would change many lives for years to come. "Justin, I have lost much, yes; but yet I have been very blessed. Mazzie has always been there for me. In those dark days it was she who willed me to live. Now, I have so much, a God fearing husband and these two angels." Miss Amelia pointed to her two sleeping sons. "My life is here now. What I want you to do with my inheritance is this."

Justin looked at his sister with anticipation.

Miss Amelia continued. "I want Mazzie to have my inheritance, all of it. Justin I ask you to protect her, as I know she is determined on returning to Richmond. Lastly, I want you both to swear to me that you will never disclose what I have told you to anyone. I do not want my beloved parents dishonored, or the memory of our lives together defamed in any manner. I will never forget what has happened to me at Everton's hand, but I have long forgiven the tortured soul."

Justin expressed no opposition to Miss Amelia's request. Though, he prudently suggested that the land ownership be transferred to Pearl rather than Mazzie. He felt the transaction would be easier to explain and defend. After Pearl's passing, Justin vowed that he and his heirs would deal with the powers that be, so as to ensure the land would be passed on the Mazzie. Mazzie would then be free to do with it as she saw fit. When the time came and Mazzie inherited the land, Justin was unconcerned over possible internal conflicts from within the Winfield family. He knew full well that Pearl had remained unmarried and that Mazzie alone gave claim as her offspring. While Miss Amelia was agreeable to Justin's suggestion, Mazzie remained uncommonly mute.

Justin spoke. "Well, Mazzie, what do you think about this arrangement?"

"Miss Amelia, I do not feel I am deserving of such generosity. You know I have always loved you, I did what I had to do."

With tears in her eyes, Miss Amelia replied. "That is why you are one of the most deserving people I have ever known. You

*never cursed me or blamed me for your lot in life; for as long as
I can remember you have been a loving and devoted sister to me.
Now, take this gift and use it to do good things for yourself and
your people."*

Soon after Justin returned to Richmond, land from Miss
Amelia's inheritance was placed in Pearl Winfield's name. Within
months of the transaction, Mazzie made her reappearance in
Charles City.

With monies from the estate, a home and barn were built
upon the land. Later, still another barn was built to accommodate
newly acquired farm animals. It would not be long before the
land and its buildings would be referred to as the Winfield Farm.
During the post war years the farm had become a safe haven for
many black folks who had been abruptly left to fend for themselves.
Much of the land had been parceled off to former slaves who
agreed to work as sharecroppers. Later the sharecropper would
be awarded ownership of that same land. This of course, was a
common practice on the larger plantations. Additional parcels of
land had been sold off, and the proceeds were used toward tuition
for those blacks aspiring to earn professional degrees.

During the early years of Winfield Farm, Mazzie opened up
her own school. There she labored day and night educating small
black children who might otherwise never have learned to read
or write. Not only were the ABC's taught, but an apprenticeship
school was begun similar to the model, Booker T. Washington
would use to establish the Tuskegee Institute in 1881.

Despite Mazzie's busy schedule, she had found time to marry
an up and coming black politician from Washington D.C., named
Randolph Hiram Cotter. She bore him a daughter and a son. Her
son and my father, Randolph Cotter Jr., stayed on at Winfield
Farm. Of course I never left either, and both my father and I
reaped the same benefits from the place as those who came before
us, had. All of this and much more, stemmed from the love,
generosity, and vision of two amazing women. Their legacy lives
on through the many lives they had touched. This very truth, as

well as my trust in the Almighty, is why, my dear lady, I leave this world not an embittered soul, but rather with great expectation.

Peace and blessings,

Samuel Cotter, M.D.

Lou's low, husky voice, perforated the silence of the chapel. "Well. there you have it; what do you think?'

Amelia felt light headed. "My head is spinning; I just can't believe that we finally know the truth. Let me sit here a minute and digest the whole thing, wow!"

"I believe I know what you are feeling, I had to reread the letter several times over, before I absorbed its essence. What struck me most was the profundity of dear Dr. Cotter's second hand account. It was as though his words crystallized the defiant grace of both women; a grace for which this sordid world had never been a match."

Remaining silent, Amelia blinked her eyes in the face of her grandmother's wisdom. She wondered when she first noticed the world's ugliness, had that benchmark occurred on September 11th, or was it much earlier? Had these hobgoblins, Sorrow and Guilt, forever stolen her joy or was there really a defiant grace? Though Amelia was well aware that Granny Lou had applied her homegrown therapy in her aid, she also believed that her grandmother trusted that she would uncover the answers to her own questions.

Lou gently nudged Amelia. "Are you with me, dear?"

"Granny Lou, what you just said is as inspiring as Dr. Cotter's letter."

Lou wrinkled her upturned nose. "Writer's license, we believe we have the duty to go on and on about anything with a hook. Seriously now, we need to look at the consequences of Dr. Cotter's decision to share his guarded secret with us."

Before Amelia could pose yet another of her percolating questions, Lou continued with her thoughtful discourse. "I'm sure the intuitive, Dr. Cotter, knew full well that through sharing this with us, he would have sowed yet another seed from the legacy of two women who died over a century ago. Though, I'm really touched by the trust he placed in us, I am somewhat ambivalent about what to do next."

Amelia knew instantly what her grandmother had been struggling with. "You mean because our gracious benefactor asked that Mazzie's account of what happened not be shared with anyone; so that means not even Mom or Granddad, right?"

"Exactly, Amelia! Throughout my marriage with your granddad the only secret we came even close to keeping was what we had bought one another for Christmas. Added to that, how can I condone asking my granddaughter to keep even relatively benign facts, from her own mother? Forgive me I am just playing the devil's advocate with myself."

Amelia's eyes sparkled and she sensed the unfamiliar gushing of endorphins through her veins. "But Granny Lou, it was really Amelia Currick Gale who decades earlier, decreed the vow of silence in order to protect the family she loved. Mazzie and Dr. Cotter were just honoring her request."

"That certainly is true. And now, just as Dr. Cotter justified his actions through reprioritizing his thinking in light of unforeseen circumstances, we are called upon to do nothing less." Lou shook her head. "Keeping the family secret is the only honorable decision available to us."

Amelia knew the tears in her grandmother's eyes mirrored her own. "Granny Lou, I am so proud of Miss Amelia and Mazzie; after all they had been through they still did right by others. I only wish that Miss Amelia had trusted Adelaide's love, enough to have shared the truth with her."

Lou vigorously blew her nose and smiled sadly. "Yes, although maybe in that event neither one of us would have been born! Oh course, that is only hypothetical. But, certainly it was tragic that Adelaide had to live her last years not knowing whether her beloved daughter was dead or alive. Fortunately, Adelaide had instilled in her young daughter a strong sense of right and wrong, and as a consequence goodness was served through the tragedy."

Amelia shook her head in agreement. "There's just one thing that bothers me about continuing to protect the Gale family name. In not disclosing the truth about the past, Mazzie will never be vindicated of wrong doing."

"I know, Amelia, I have thought long and hard about that aspect of the situation. It's rather ironic that Amelia Currick Gale's wishes for Everton's sins to remain buried had become Mazzie's and her grandson's wish, as well. I do believe the saving grace had been Justin Gale's actions. His behavior said more than words ever could to vindicate Mazzie in the eyes of public opinion. Clearly, it would have been bizarre for a man to protect the woman if he believed she had brought harm to a beloved sibling."

Understanding her grandmother's reasoning, Amelia nodded in agreement. "I guess, little good would come from sharing the history with the Bissetts?"

Lou did not mince words. "I believe even though the events took place over a century and a half ago, the truth would accomplish little save to embarrass the Gale-Bissett family. As it stands, the family remains a figure head of the community, having had to work hard to atone for a history in which their forebears had perpetuated slavery. Though blameless for the past, I'm sure they would feel unnecessary shame if forced to reconcile Everton's sins, as well. I think this would be the case even if the information were to be shared only with the family."

Lou paused a moment to gaze at the luminous stain glass window. "Sitting here today reaffirms my conviction that our forebears never really leave us at all, for better or for worse, we leave them."

Amelia considered the truth behind her grandmother's words. "I guess, we've opened Pandora's Box, or should I say Dr. Cotter's letter. Now, along with Dr. Cotter and the rest of the well meaning busybodies, we are destined to be the protectors of Amelia Currick Gale's guarded secret." The teenager cupped her grandmother's right hand within her own as though to make a pact.

Lou was about to respond, when their conversation was interrupted by the grinding sound of gravel from the outside parking lot. "That must be the workmen returning; I think we should leave."

Lou and Amelia closed the chapel door behind them and walked but two steps before encountering two, well seasoned, workmen. With a pleasant smile the older worker greeted the women. "Good afternoon, what brings you ladies to this out of the way place?"

Lou and Amelia returned the greeting and added that they had just stopped for a quiet lunch under the trees. Lou inquired. "Are you repairing the old chapel so it might be opened to the public?"

Once again the older man spoke. "Well if hearsay has it right, Covenant Presbyterian plans to reopen the site for both its historical significance as well as for an alternate sanctuary. I guess this would be the perfect setting for a wedding or that type of thing. Would you like to take a peek inside?" As he spoke he placed his hand upon the door latch. To his chagrin he discovered that the door had been left unlocked. In annoyance, he turned to the younger man standing beside him. "Hey Joe, you forgot to lock the door; we could have lost all our tools!"

Before the men exchanged another word, Lou thanked the workman for his invitation and she and Amelia took their leave. As they distanced themselves from the chapel, Amelia's stomach growled, reminding her that it was well past the lunch hour. Feeling genuinely uncertain of what might follow, she petitioned her grandmother. "Well, are we still going to have our picnic?"

"I don't know how you feel, but for me a picnic would be anticlimactic! How about, we briefly visit with Amelia Currick Gale and the rest of the clan, and then head for home. If you are famished, we can eat our lunch in the car while driving." Lou searched Amelia's face for a consensus of opinion.

Though her stomach continued to complain, she was open to a change of plans. The past hour and a half had given Amelia much to think about. Though happy that the family mystery had been solved, once again, a thrust of adult decisions had fractured her peace. She was more than ready to return to New Haven. Angelically, Amelia smiled at her grandmother. "That sounds positively perfect!"

CHAPTER 17

Lost and Found

Labor Day, September 2003, came and went. New Haven High School, once again, opened its doors to students. The sound of a car horn set Amelia's departure into motion. "Bye Mom, I have to go!" Quickly, though no less affectionately, Amelia brushed the side of her mother's cheek with a kiss.

"Do you have money for lunch?" Before the words left her lips, Karen remembered she had given Amelia money the evening before.

"Yes, Mom, remember?"

"Okay, yes, I do; now please be careful! Tell Trish to go easy on the gas-pedal!" Karen anxiously watched as her daughter, no longer a child, hurried out the door. It was of little consolation that Trish had a respectable driving record. Since her husband's death, as hard as she tried, Karen had difficulty controlling her urge to overprotect Amelia.

Tears welled in her eyes as she watched the teen make her way confidently down the front steps. How she wished Ken had lived to watch their daughter's metamorphosis into such a lovely young woman. It was times like this, when Karen would force herself to recount the lessons of her childhood. From the depth of her soul, she murmured, *"Oh ye of little faith!"*

She remembered her parent's quoting scripture with the assurance that human consciousness survives the grave. Those thoughts alone lifted her spirits, never failing to clarify for her that Ken knew full well how both she and Amelia had fared since without his physical presence. Yet the void remained, and she realized, she had never been fully prepared for the uncompromising finality of Ken's untimely death. Strong faith aside, she feared that as long as life was hers she would always have an empty place in her heart.

Vacillating as she would, Karen always returned to her well learned pragmatism. A pragmatism which afforded her a graceful rebound from her many slumps. She realized that since that fateful day two years earlier, she and Amelia had come a long way toward healing. She was both grateful to her God, and proud that they had somehow survived.

The front door closed behind the doting mother, as she hurried to answer the telephone's demanding ring. Karen muttered aloud. "It's a good thing I did not go to work today!"

"Hello! Oh, Mom, you must have ESP. How did you know I would be home?"

"Karen, you had mentioned it last week. I thought you might be interested in having lunch, my treat?"

"Mom, you are an angel for asking, but I can't. I need to catch up on some cataloging that I have not been able to get to while at work."

"Well, okay then, some other time." Lou jumped to her next question. "Are you still planning to attend the 9/11 anniversary service at Grace Presbyterian, this year?"

As though speaking to herself Karen's voice trailed off. "Yes, we will not attend the ground zero memorial service this year. Florence and Frank will be joining us at Grace

Presbyterian. I can hardly believe Ken is gone two years. I just hope and pray that the resurgence of memories from that day does not reverse the positive changes I have seen in Amelia, these past six months."

Lou sounded typically upbeat. "Yes, it seems as though Amelia has rejoined the living. Why, the last time I spoke with her she was going on and on about her activities at school and talked incessantly about her old friends."

Karen interjected. "For this I am very grateful, but I am still very concerned. This morning she left for school with a bounce in her step, while last evening she was an entirely different person. It is like I am living with my sweet daughter one moment and a bedeviled adolescent the next!"

"Why, what did Amelia do last evening that has caused you so much concern?"

Karen grimaced. "I know what you are thinking, Mom, but I am not making a big deal out of nothing. I overheard Amelia playing a new piece last evening; it was so beautiful. When I entered the room, she immediately stopped. I did not succeed in hiding my frustration. I confronted her and asked why she had stopped playing her soulful music. At which point, she began jabbering about a multitude of unrelated topics. I had to leave the room, so I would not scream at her to stop and answer me!" Karen waited for what seemed an eternity before her mother replied.

"I can only imagine how hard this has been for you, Karen, but you may just have to accept that perhaps our prodigy may not want to pursue a career in music!"

Karen felt the veins in her neck bulge, while her voice welled with frustration. "Mom, that may be the case, but if not music than what? Though she continues to excel at her schoolwork, she remains resistant to constructively planning for her future. To be specific, she continually procrastinates in submitting college applications. If Amelia has selected a new course of study, she has certainly not shared that information with me."

"My dear, dear, girl, you have discussed this with me verbatim and I know you have confided in Dr. Beale, as well; the answer is always the same. Even a teenager who has not suffered the emotional trauma our Amelia has, will often be uncertain and hesitant in making life choices."

Almost in tears, Karen's voice moved up an octave. "Oh, Mom, I am so very proud of her already; I just want her to be happy and fulfilled. Her behavior is so uncharacteristic for either a McDowell or a Morelli!"

"Yes, but she is Amelia, first. If you don't calm down I will be crying as well. I tell you that our girl will get through this and when she does she will need her mother to be there with her. Now, as your mother, I insist that you take care of yourself, and have faith in your wonderful daughter. Remember, our Lord always has a plan; it will be okay!"

Karen placed the phone back upon the receiver and vowed to adhere to her mother's sound advice. She rationalized that the resurgence of many of her fears, were directly related to the fast approaching second anniversary of her husband's death.

*   *   *   *

September 11th arrived without further incident. As planned, Frank and Florence Morelli arrived at their daughter-in-law's home by 4:30 PM. Lou and Mike had arrived earlier, and were present to greet the couple. Over the years the in-laws had developed a deep love and respect for one another. Ken's untimely death had served to bond the families even closer together. Tears and memories, only scratched the surface of the emotional web spun following the 9/11 tragedy. Both families realized and cherished their indelible connection with one another.

As Karen prepared for her guests she felt as though her stomach had been turned inside out. Yet, bravely she entertained her kin. "I thought you might like some hors d'oeuvres to hold you over until our dinner following the church service. We have Brie and crackers, and of course I did not forget Grand Papa's anchovies."

"Oh, *bella mia,* Karen you are a sucha angel! Speaking ofa angels where a is mya precious granddaughter?"

"I really do not have a clue; she raced out of here at the sound of Trish's horn. On the way out, she said she would meet us at church. Your angel, Grand Papa, is making me into a nervous wreck!" Karen looked clearly perplexed.

To Karen's dismay, Frank refused to let the topic of discussion end. "Do you thinka perhaps thea service might bea too much a for her and she isa looking a fora easy way out?"

Lou immediately responded. "Frank, I am certain Amelia would have told her mother if she was not planning to attend the service."

"Yes, you are right, Mom." Karen's face relaxed, her mother's words quelling her worse fear.

Frank smiled in good humor. "I knowa better then to argue witha two women. Mike, pleasea pass mea those anchovies!"

Florence appeared to have sensed the tension in the room, as she quickly changed the subject. "Lou, I havea been meaning to ask ayou howa your ancestral search has abeen going; have youa completed thea project?"

Lou immediately perked up. "Well, a matter of fact, we did complete the project and I believe it has been a worthwhile experience for both Amelia and myself."

Florence continued. "I spokea with Amelia about thea search shortly after you and a she returned from Virginia. She said that a you were acertain that Amelia Currick Gale, I believe thata is the name, had been the ancestral grandmother fora whom shea had been named. Amelia seemed a genuinely excited about this and a even mentioned thata she would likea to begin a genealogy search on the Morelli side of thea family."

"Yes, it had taken many hours of research by Matt, Amelia and myself. But, that is precisely what we had discovered." Lou beamed.

Frank interjected. "Lou, I have toa hand it toa you. When I firsta heard about your idea I believed youa didn't have both youra ores in the water, if youa geta my drift. But ita worked! I havea seen a world ofa difference in oura girl; she isa slowly returning to her, how doa you say, vivacious self. If wea had only a known thea outcome, Karen could havea saved the thousands of dollars spenta on Dr. Beale!"

Lou smiled broadly. "Thank you, Frank, you flatter me. I certainly cannot accept all the credit you are giving me. We have all put aside our own hurt to help pull Amelia through this. And mind you, our Lord and Dr. Beale have always been on our side."

Karen hung on every word, before her compulsion to bring everyone back to her own reality got the best of her. "Unfortunately, we are not out of the woods yet!"

Frank looked at his daughter in-law with the slightest hint of frustration. "Oh, yes, shea still does not playa the piano and shea has yet toa decide upon a college."

A disconcerting silence fell upon the room, until with dry humor, Mike salvaged the moment. "For me, I vote with Frank, I think Lou has done a wonderful job with our darling Amelia. Both she, and my fretting daughter are nothing short of amazing."

Mike succeeded in getting a smile from everyone, even Karen, who was beginning to show the strain of the occasion.

Mike continued. "Well, don't you think we better get going, it is already, 5:30 PM. We still have to meet the rest of the gang at the church. I'm certain the service will be packed."

*   *   *   *

Karen buried her clammy cold hands within the warm pockets of her quilted camel colored jacket. Stepping from her father's car, she craned her neck in search of Amelia. The rest of the family made their way into the church.

Many others headed toward the church. The large attendance served as a cold reminder of the many New Haven residents who had experienced personal loss, or knew of someone who had died in the September 11th attack.

Karen began to climb the steps leading into the stately Gothic church. Her head was spinning. She steadied herself against the large Doric pillars lining the front of the sanctuary. When her legs buckled for a third time, to her relief a strong supporting arm took hold of her.

"Are you okay, Sis? Where is the rest of the family?"

Karen turned to find her brother Alex, standing behind her. With him were his wife Pat, Matt, and a pretty wide eyed girl. "Alex, I'm so glad to see you all here, everyone is already in the church staking out a pew for us. Everyone, that is, except Amelia; have you run into her by any chance?"

Alex shook his head. "I'm sure Amelia will show up sooner or later. It is getting late we had better join the others inside the church. Oh, Karen, let me introduce you to Lisa Singer. Matt and Lisa drove all the way from Virginia to share this day with us."

Karen warmly embraced Lisa and the others, before reluctantly entering the church. Stifling tears, she seated herself between her mother and mother-in-law. In silence she sat, unable to erase an image of Amelia crouched in a corner, unable to face another memorial service with her family.

The magnificent pipe organ resonated within the large stone structure. At the close of Susan D. Wiseman's memorial piece, *God Will Prevail*, senior pastor Dr. Stephen Ramson began with a short prayer and welcome. The minister's electrifying words lifted Karen and the family to heights not experienced in a very long time. "If you have looked at the program guide for this service, you realize how blessed we are that so many individuals were willing to share their talents with us this evening. Just like yourselves, they are here to pay tribute to those that left us on 9/11. There is one more name that did not make it into our program guide. Only last week, our dedicated organist and choir director, Martha Tuttle, asked if we could add another performer to the program. Of course, the program guide had already been printed, that being enough to send any good Presbyterian into anaphylactic shock. Still, due to the circumstances, we found within ourselves the spontaneity necessary to work the young lady into the service. I believe you will agree we made the right decision. Now, while you will not find her name in your program, our own Ms. Amelia Morelli will begin the service with the classical piece *Memorial 5-9/11/01,* written by Edward Gold, an alumnus of Yale University, School of Music. She will also serve as accompanist to the Grace Presbyterian chorus in the closing hymn, *Find Us Faithful,* by Jon Mohr. My sincere thanks, once again, to all our participants. Your music lifts us beyond the pain of loss, enabling us to celebrate everything our loved ones ever were, and continue to be. Thanks, be, to our Lord and Savior Jesus Christ."

Karen, oblivious to her family's stupefied grins and tears, took a deep breath as Amelia began to perform. Slowly, she breathed, exhaling upon every solid note her daughter played. Amelia sat poised, once again the seasoned pianist Ken and Karen had nurtured over the years. To Karen's mind, her daughter appeared nothing less than ethereal in her simple long sleeved white and silver satin dress. Amelia's only adornment, the same masculine cross given her by Stew Dempsey.

A deafening silence followed the performance. After a long pause, Pastor Ramson's baritone voice broke the spell; alphabetically he began to speak the names of those local individuals who had died on 9/11. Karen closed her eyes and listened in anticipation for her husband's name. The sound of

Ken's name spoken, loud and strong, *Kenneth Frank Morelli,* seemed to give him new breath, and she knew at that moment he was not merely a memory. She felt joy in that everyone in the sanctuary would know that Ken had once known life and continued to live, not only for those who loved and missed him. The simultaneous touch of Lou and Florence, sweet though distracting, reminded Karen that she had never been alone in her grief. She remembered how these strong women had suffered their own pain. Yet in that moment she could neither share her thoughts, nor console them, for fear of losing the scant composure left to her.

The rest of the service, though far surpassing Karen's expectations, seemed endless. All she hoped for was that Amelia would once again take the stage. After what seemed an eternity, the girl seated herself at the piano. Karen felt her body stiffen. "Dear Lord, please give Amelia the strength to play as flawlessly as she had earlier." Karen believed her prayer was answered, when the crystal clear notes preceded the harmony of the chorus. Thereafter, the poignant words of the Jon Mohr hymn, *Find Us Faithful,* mystically transcended the sound of the piano, even for Karen.

O may all who come behind us find us faithful,
May the fire of our devotion light their way,
May the footprints that we leave lead them to believe, and the lives
we live inspire them to obey.
O may all who come behind us find us faithful.

Unabashed, Karen blew her nose, while tears of joy softly tracked down her cheeks. Lou and Florence held her close on either side. With emotions stripped raw, the family stood in silence, discreetly wiping the tears from their eyes.

Aging, Pastor Ramson's deep voice, once again brought his flock back from their introspection. With conviction and passion he spoke his closing words. "My brethren, let us go in peace and in celebration of the lives lost that sorrowful day two years ago. Remain confident that we shall meet again in the victory afforded us all, through our Lord and Savor Jesus Christ. Now, let us not disappoint Him or our loved ones; live your God given lives in goodness and in love! Amen."

A mood of unity swept through the sanctuary and Karen no longer felt the isolation she experienced only an hour earlier. With the rest of the congregation, in silence and with eyes glazed, Karen filed out of the sanctuary. She and her family slowly moved toward the church courtyard. For several minutes Karen's eyes darted through the crowd in search of Amelia's face. It was not long before she found herself in the grip of resurging anxiety. "I hope Amelia remembers that we are dining out; I'll go see if she is dawdling in the choir room."

"Aunt Karen, Lisa and I will go. I'd like to introduce Lisa to Amelia before we head back to Virginia."

Karen's resolve to find Amelia softened in the face of Matt's earnest willingness to assist her. "Ah, well, maybe it will take the tenacity of youth to track her down. Don't you and Lisa get lost and forget to come back!"

"Don't worry, Mrs. Morelli, we will find her!" Lisa turned and smiled as she followed Matt toward the church annex.

The rest of the family conversed with one another as they waited within the church courtyard. Pat turned to Karen. "We are all so proud of Amelia; her performance was nothing short of amazing."

Karen beamed, shaking her head in affirmation. "Yes, I am as proud as a Mama can be, though I remain cautiously optimistic. Remember, that of late Amelia comes with an arsenal of surprises."

Pat and Alex grimaced. "Don't, they all! We just learned that not only will we be planning for a graduation this spring, but a wedding as well."

The corners of Karen's mouth turned upward into a wide

grin. "How wonderful; Lisa seems so lively, a good match for our sensitive Matt!"

Alex concurred. "We certainly understand why Matt is so smitten. Lisa is all you could ask for in a prospective daughter-in-law; a bright and lovely girl from an accomplished Richmond family."

Pat hesitated. "Our only concern is the religious difference; Lisa is from a practicing Jewish family."

Karen pressed her lips tight together as she fought to control the grin ready to explode across her face. She was quick to note the Mona Lisa smiles upon the faces of the rest of the family.

Lou philosophically interjected. "The longer I hang around, the more I question the cookie cutter recipe for a good marriage and happiness. Maybe, if you start out with a healthy mix of love and respect, you end up okay!"

"Lou, I don'ta know exactly what ayou are a getting at but here comes one of mya reasons to bea happy!" Frank pointed out the three young faces moving through the dwindling crowd.

Before Karen could move, the family hovered around the willowy teenager, showing little reserve in expressing their love and pride in her accomplishment. Karen watched, while Amelia subjected herself to a barrage of hugs and kisses. She thought her daughter showed the patience of an old soul, while in quiet submission to her family's praise. As Amelia opened her mouth to speak, Karen noted a renegade tear in the corner of the girl's eye. "So, I guess I did okay; that was for Dad."

CHAPTER 18
Fruit of the Tree

Before rolling out of bed, Amelia stretched her long delicate arms high above her head. Only a week before her seventeenth birthday, and Amelia felt certain she had already exhausted the processing capacity of her zillion and some brain cells. On some level of her being, she resented the way in which the trauma of the past few years had taken its toll upon her once carefree life. Thankful for small blessings, she was relieved that this year's birthday celebration would be on a far smaller scale than last year's lavish party. Granny Lou and her granddad would be hosting the gathering, and only family and close friends were invited.

Chiming punctually at 9:00 AM, the hall clock reminded Amelia of the day's mission. Frenzied, she pulled her baggy Yale shirt over her head and squeezed into her stretch blue jeans. Once dressed, she bounded down the stairs and flew into the kitchen where she expected to find her mom. There was no sign of her mother and the kitchen took on a bare and empty look. Amelia missed the aroma of fresh brewed coffee, as well as the welcoming bowl of one of her mom's concocted mega grain cereals. A sudden chill traveled down her spine; just for a fleeting moment she imagined how unbearable it would be if her mom were ever lost to her. A sense of urgency spoke to her. How Amelia regretted the heartache she was certain she had caused her mother over the past two years. Why today, the very day she planned to make amends, was her mom absent from the only room in the house where she could always be found this hour of the morning?

In a gallop, Amelia returned to the second floor and searched her mother's bedroom and bath. Finding the rooms empty, the girl returned to the first level of the house. Stealth-like she made her way to the back of the home. With profound relief Amelia found her mother dreamily sitting in the sun room. Bending over the lonely woman, she planted a soft kiss upon her forehead. Before words were exchanged, Amelia gracefully moved her svelte body to the chair opposite her mother. "What dream have I caught you in?"

"Oh, Amelia, you move like a cat. I didn't even hear you behind me. I thought since this is Saturday, that you might have plans. So, I didn't bother making either of us breakfast."

"Well, there is absolutely nothing on my calendar for today. In fact, I was thinking that maybe, together we could tackle cleaning up the garage. There are things we haven't touched since Dad…" Amelia stopped and searched her mother's face.

"Amelia, am I hearing you correctly? You actually want to spend your Saturday cleaning up the garage with your mother, absolutely amazing!"

"Oh Mom, isn't that, what is that favorite word of yours? I have it, hyperbole!"

Karen wrinkled up her brow as though in deep thought. "Well, maybe just a little. Actually, I had been toying with hiring someone to do the dirty job, with your help that wouldn't be necessary. Besides, it is probably better if we do it ourselves; we would not want anything of importance to get lost in the cleanup, would we now?"

Amelia smiled weakly. "No Mom, we would not. Well, let's grab something to eat and get started!"

*　　*　　*　　*

At the sight of the cluttered garage, Karen shuddered. "Are you sure you are up to this?"

Amelia arched her dark brows. "Definitely, let's go. You know after looking for ghosts in Granny Lou's attic over the past year, I am more than ready to face this garage."

Together, mother and daughter began sifting through the garage shelves. Amelia realized that much of her mom and dad's college memorabilia had been stored on these same shelves. From time to time, she glanced at her mother's face, certain that a year earlier, neither one of them would have been able to undertake the heart-wrenching task.

"Okay, just stop, we need a plan before we go any further with this. First, Amelia, take my car keys and get this car out of here. When you come back I will tell you what we are going to do." The renewed authority in her mother's voice gave Amelia the confidence that they would complete the task before them. With a smile on her face, she willingly followed her mother's directives.

When she returned to the garage, Amelia found that her mom had placed two large signs at the opposite sides of the garage. One sign read *TRASH PILE*, while the other *KEEPER PILE*.

"This is what we are going to do! We simply box accordingly; if there is any question as to where something belongs, we will consult. Amelia, let's take advantage of your height; you take the higher shelves, here is the stepladder. While Shorty, yours truly, will take the lower shelves." Karen grinned widely at Amelia. "Just be careful on that ladder."

Amelia grimaced. "This is just like old times, isn't it, Mom?"

As the day progressed, items retrieved from the shelves

included old pamphlets and photos, trophies, sports equipment, football memorabilia and automobile parts. Shelf by shelf, all items were examined and at times discussed in length. Predictably, many more items found their way into the keeper pile than into the trash pile.

Stepping from the ladder's lofty perch, Amelia carefully placed one of her father's debating trophies into the keeper pile. In the softest whisper, Amelia spoke. "I guess a family is blessed when most of their things go into the keeper pile, rather than the trash; don't you think, Mom?"

With tears rolling down her cheeks Karen reached out for Amelia. "Oh, yes dear, I certainly do agree!"

Amelia fell into her mother's arms, not so much seeking comfort as to render it. The girl pulled a wad of tissues from her jean pocket and wiped away her mother's tears. "Mom, if I decided to go to college would we be able to manage without Dad's support?"

Amelia felt her mother's body stiffen, while at the same time her face looked unmistakably, dumbfounded. "Why, Amelia, with your dad's life insurance and the government settlement, we have more than enough to send you wherever you might choose to go. In addition, your dad and I had put money aside specifically for your education. The plan was that you would receive the first of two checks on your seventeenth birthday, and the second at your High School graduation. Amelia, we are very blessed to have these resources. My goodness, is that why you have procrastinated in applying to Julliard?"

Though well rehearsed, Amelia felt her chest fill with emotion. "No, that is not the reason!"

Karen shook as she spoke. "Then what is it? You use to be able to tell your dad and me everything that was bothering you. Amelia, please tell me what has changed that?"

"I, I wanted to tell you for so long; I just felt so ashamed of myself!" In a fit of catharsis, Amelia continued. "The very day of the tragedy, I had planned to talk with you both, when you and Dad returned from work. I was prepared to confess to you my doubts about pursuing a music career. I just wanted to be free to explore all the many other exciting things in life! It was so hard when I remembered how you and Dad had sacrificed: the money for piano lessons, running me around for recitals, and you never missed one of my performances. After all you had done for me that was what I was going to tell you."

Though the words continued to form in Amelia's head, their vocalization proved nothing short of climbing Mount Everest. "After Dad died so suddenly, I could barely look at the piano, much less play it. I began to believe that Dad was taken from me as a punishment for the disappointment I was about to inflict upon you both. I know this sounds ridiculous, but it felt like I had somehow caused his death."

Her mother's thin arms never felt stronger as they wrapped her into a tight embrace. "Oh, my poor child, please understand you had absolutely nothing to do with your father's death. And besides, our loving God would never do such a terrible thing. As for your decision to forego a music career, I must ask you to forgive both your dad and me for not communicating how much you have always meant to us. You know Amelia, when you were a tiny baby, your dad and I did not know exactly what you were going to look like, whether you would be smart, or for that matter if you might end up a musical prodigy. All we knew was that you were ours, and we loved you more than anything else in this world. I imagine, in the same way our Heavenly Father in heaven loves us all. Because our love for you has never changed, we only wanted you to do and be whatever made you the happiest. If through the process of living, we somehow lost sight of our daughter, and only saw the amazingly talented girl we believed lived for her music, Amelia, I am truly sorry." Karen sighed long and hard. "Even when we start out with the best of intentions, it seems we humans get things especially jumbled up when it comes to those we love the most."

When her mother finished speaking, Amelia felt a new sense of appreciation for how challenging it must be to raise a child. Her mind flashed back to the sad story of the Gale family, and at that moment, it was as though she felt not only her mother's pain but Adelaide's pain as well. "Mom, you and Dad did nothing wrong; I don't know why it has taken me so long to trust you with my truth. I only wish that Amelia Currick Gale had trusted Adelaide with her truth before it was too late. Granny Lou said that despite all the bad things that had happened to the Gale family, that good eventually came out of it. Still, I don't understand why innocent people have to suffer the way Adelaide and Amelia Currick Gale, had."

"Well, Amelia, this world has not been perfect for a very long time. Even so we are promised that if we trust in the Lord, He will take all the broken pieces of our lives and create something more spectacular than you or I could ever imagine. I truly believe that whatever your namesake's truth might have been, Adelaide has all the answers she needs now, and is at peace. To her great credit she raised a daughter who was able to rise above her circumstances and live a life of love and giving. In fact, not too long ago, this wise old mother told me, that God always has a plan."

Amelia knowingly, laughed. "You wouldn't be speaking of Granny Lou, would you?"

Karen returned Amelia's smile. "None, other!"

"Mom, I'm not quite finished, there is more. I've been accepted for next year's fall enrollment at Yale. Uncle Stew helped me with the application, and last week I received my letter of acceptance. Well, what do you think?"

Karen just stared at her daughter, looking as though she had been struck by a dozen moonbeams, all at the same time. Though her lips moved she remained speechless, while tears trickled down her cheeks.

Amelia nervously laughed. "Mom, do your tears mean you are happy or sad?

Karen pulled her daughter closer, so close that Amelia could feel the wetness of her mother's tears. This time, when her mother's lips parted, she spoke the words Amelia had so very much wanted to hear. "I'm so very happy for the both of us. As for your dad, it is as though he were whispering in my ear as we speak."

"Mom, don't joke about something like that! So, what is he saying?"

"He wants me to tell you that he loves you very much. He has asked me to speak aloud Psalms 48:14, *For this is God, our God forever and ever; he will be our guide even unto death.*"

Life can only be understood backwards,
But it must be lived forwards.

Soren Kierkgaard

Jane Amelia Smith, afterthoughts

As my virginal plunge into that broad expanse of professional writers and publishers, I chose to write about the great equalizer, death. Though a gloomy beginning, certainly a part of life we will all experience.

Death has been no stranger to my household. Over the course of recent years, I have lost my father and a close college friend to illness, and my husband through a tragic accident. Actually, this book was written for the benefit of the author, as well as the reader. The only prerequisite for this reading remains earthly mortality.

When I began writing, I intended for my protagonist, Amelia, to represent the 3,300 children who lost parents in the terrorist attack on September 11, 2001. For the most part, their stories will remain untold. Hidden from public domain, there is little doubt that through the ensuing silent years, they have endured their own unique struggles. The consequential loose ends of their lives, dealt with by themselves and their loved ones. Now, over a decade removed from that day of carnage, their lives remain a quiet testament to God and themselves.

After I finished the novel, I realized that my heroine is not solely representative of the innocents affected that tragic day. I know now, that Amelia represents all those survivors joined together in that nameless mosaic of human suffering and triumph. She represents those who courageously live and love as our Heavenly Father intended. Then, when the time comes, as it surely will, death is faced head on. Yes, the grief is cutting, but the still confidence that our Lord and Savior will always have the last word, remains. If this story reminds you of what the Christian faith brings to the table in times of troubled waters, I have succeeded. Indeed, I would be uncommonly blessed, should the pages of this book deliver the reader to a higher truth, than that of our own.

CPSIA information can be obtained at www.ICGtesting.com
Printed in the USA
BVOW020924170512

290419BV00001B/1/P